ABRACADABRA
STREET

ABRACADABRA
STREET

MARK ROLAND LANGDALE

Copyright © 2022 Mark Roland Langdale

The moral right of the author has been asserted.

Apart from any fair dealing for the purposes of research or private study, or criticism or review, as permitted under the Copyright, Designs and Patents Act 1988, this publication may only be reproduced, stored or transmitted, in any form or by any means, with the prior permission in writing of the publishers, or in the case of reprographic reproduction in accordance with the terms of licences issued by the Copyright Licensing Agency. Enquiries concerning reproduction outside those terms should be sent to the publishers.

Matador
Unit E2 Airfield Business Park,
Harrison Road, Market Harborough,
Leicestershire. LE16 7UL
Tel: 0116 2792299
Email: books@troubador.co.uk
Web: www.troubador.co.uk/matador
Twitter: @matadorbooks

ISBN 978 1803132 778

British Library Cataloguing in Publication Data.
A catalogue record for this book is available from the British Library.

Printed and bound in the UK by TJ Books Limited, Padstow, Cornwall
Typeset in 12pt Adobe Jenson Pro by Troubador Publishing Ltd, Leicester, UK

Matador is an imprint of Troubador Publishing Ltd

To Vern (Langdale) my brother and my best friend and to all the girls and boys at Troubador. Special thanks to Andrea and Fern. Also to Briony and Esther Harvey and finally to Davenport Magic Shop the oldest magic shop in the world.

In memory of my dear friend Gilly (Norwood)
– The spirit lives on.

Prologue

What do you do if the family business is magic – being magicians and builders of tricks and illusions for other magicians – and you're all fingers and thumbs? Do you turn your back on magic and walk away, as far away from Abracadabra Street as you can? Or do you try to overcome the hand you're dealt, a hand of jokers, so one day you can become an ace magician like Merlin the Magician, Robert Houdin, the King of Conjurers, Harry Houdini, Illusionist and Escapologist Extraordinaire, or Blackstone, the Master Magician – no relation to the boy in this story, Benjamin Blackstone, I hasten to add.

This was the question Benjamin Blackstone was now asking himself, hiding away in the attic of his mind. Benjamin wished he lived in a house with a magical attic for he was sure if this was the case he would, as if by magic, be transformed into the greatest magician of all time. Unfortunately for Benjamin, this was wishful thinking on a grand scale. Captain Hook, a man who most certainly did not have the magic touch, had more chance than Benjamin Blackstone of earning a living as a magician

'If only I could do magic,' sighed Benjamin, staring wistfully out of the skylight window, the one his father had put into the loft space, a poor man's – poor boy's – attic in Benjamin's mind. Still, it was nice of his parents to try and give him the magical space he had always dreamt of. The family magic business had taken a turn for the worse, dark magic, in no small way brought on by Benjamin's great-grandfather Atticus Blackstone, the black sheep of the family. The family story went that Atticus turned bad after he found out to his cost that, like Benjamin, he wasn't cut out for the magic trade. Atticus Blackstone, desperate and one step from the poorhouse, sold the family secrets – a cardinal sin in all magic circles and one that got the Blackstones thrown out of the famed Magic Circle in London. Being thrown out of the Magic Circle virtually ruined the family business. Unable to perform on the magic circuit, all that was left was to sell their illusions and magic tricks, mostly in Europe, for no magician or conjurer in their right mind who was a member of the esteemed Magic Circle in London wanted to be associated with the Blackstone family name, blackened as it was.

Over time, the Blackstone name blackened to charcoal black, bone black, some said. But Atticus Blackstone began to become a lighter shade of black, almost grey, as in the grey areas of life, although very little is ever black and white in the theatre of life. There was even talk of the Magic Circle, who once upon a time had blackballed the Blackstone family, inviting them back into their famed circle of magic.

Benjamin had heard a family story, and a most magical one, of his great-grandfather buying a book on the subject of magic in an antiquarian bookstore in the backstreets of Budapest in Hungary. You see, one of Atticus Blackstone's heroes was the magician Erich Weiss, aka Harry Houdini. The book, a Victorian popup book of a street on which a long line of magic shops sat, was named *Abracadabra Street*. This street certainly had a magical ring to it, as magic rings (otherwise known as miracle rings) had when you rubbed them together, like music to the ears, as a stage act in the music-hall days of Vaudeville London might have performed back in the times of the Victorians and Edwardians.

The Victorian popup book was said to be magical in some way, or so the antiquarian wizened owner of the bookshop had told Atticus, after which he issued his great-grandfather a note of caution: 'Be careful…' To which Atticus was said to have jumped in with the well-worn magical line, 'What you wish for.'

'If you would do me the courtesy of allowing me to finish my sentence,' scowled the wizened old man, 'be careful you don't get trapped in any illusion you cannot escape from as I can see you are no Harry Houdini,' the man added, appearing to see right through Atticus Blackstone as if he were a ghost.

The more likely story was that Atticus Blackstone was so shallow that the man instantly saw through him, saw him for what he was: a scoundrel. However, the owner of the magic shop, Magica's Magic Box, had fallen upon hard times and as Atticus had given him three gold sovereigns, three being the magic number, he felt he had no choice but to sell the book. The only reason Atticus Blackstone found himself on East St was because he had picked a pocket or three in the city of Budapest on his way to the magic shop.

Atticus didn't quite know what to make of this warning but brushed it off as the ramblings of an old man, so he bought the book and walked out of the shop as if he were a giant and one carrying a street under his arm: Abracadabra Street. If this book was indeed magical in some way, Atticus Blackstone may one day become one of the giants of magic, right up there with Harry Houdin and Jean-Eugène Robert-Houdin.

The old book must have been magical in some way for it turned Benjamin's great-grandfather into a household name in Europe, a giant in the circles in which magicians circulated. That was until, once again, for the second time, his great-grandfather turned bad, ending up on the dark end of Magic Street. The book was said to have possessed Atticus, or perhaps it was the spirit that haunted the book that had possessed Atticus Blackstone. Either way, Atticus ended up almost losing his mind until finally he came to his senses and threw the book on the open fire. Later, Atticus became a recluse in an old ramshackle mansion house in the country.

When Atticus Blackstone died, he bequeathed the house to the Blackstone family in his last will and testament but the Blackstone family wanted nothing to do with the old mansion house, feeling Atticus had bought it with money earned on the black market, blood money in some cases. Benjamin, being a curious sort of boy, wanted to see where his great-grandfather – as bad as a magician as himself – lived, so one day, against his parents' wishes, Benjamin set out to find the house.

1

Attic Magic

'Wow, what a monster of a house – a broken-down monster – let's hope it doesn't wake up any time soon,' exclaimed Benjamin, talking out loud as he walked up the broken-down steps and past the sunken garden as the old house revealed itself as if by magic – a giant conjuring trick. As if the house itself was a giant Victorian pop-up book. You see, the old house was surrounded by tall trees, which meant from the village you couldn't see the old mansion house. 'You can't see the wood for the trees,' was an old expression which had curiously popped out of Benjamin's head only a few moments earlier.

'There must be a magical attic at the top of the house, an attic fit for any magician worth his salt; if I can't do magic in the attic then I can't do magic,' Benjamin continued, sure he was the only one around, apart from the birds and the wild animals, which lived in the surrounding woodland that encircled the house like a giant green magic circle.

Benjamin entered the house without any difficulty; the large wooden oak front door wasn't locked, in fact it was slightly ajar, as if someone was expecting him, probably the local ghost. The local ghost no doubt was his great-grandfather, Atticus Blackstone, the black sheep of the family according to his parents. If this was indeed the case then he should expect some nasty surprises of the dark magic variety. But Benjamin wasn't scared; he didn't believe in ghosts, spooks and all that nonsense; they only existed in the supernatural world of the Victorian ghost story. Benjamin only believed in one thing: MAGIC with a big M. Unfortunately for Benjamin, magic with a small m didn't appear to believe in him. Or perhaps it was because Benjamin didn't really believe in himself and, as such, magic didn't believe in him; or couldn't, for life, the universe and everything in between only responded to positive energy. No matter how much Benjamin's parents and his teachers told him he should believe in himself, somehow he couldn't quite make himself believe this was true.

Being a magician was all about self-belief and making others believe in the unbelievable; all great magicians had an aura which surrounded them – a magical aura just like a magic circle. You most certainly couldn't pull this trick off if you didn't believe in yourself. No wonder Benjamin Blackstone was a lousy magician. This lack of confidence soon became evident when he stepped onto a stage, materialising in the physical form of his body not doing what he wished it would do. It was as if he was being possessed by a malevolent poltergeist as the cards in his hands flew into the audience in anything but a magical way as Benjamin tripped over his feet and his tongue at the same time. This made Benjamin wish he had the power of invisibility like the great magician and illusionist Harry Potter. It wasn't simply because Benjamin got stage fright, which he did, for these sorts of things happened even when he was practising cards tricks and magical illusions in his bedroom.

'Welcome to my Theatre of Magic,' a disembodied voice cried out in a theatrical manner as Benjamin stopped dead in his tracks at the foot of the winding staircase. *It must be the wind whistling through the door*, thought Benjamin; alternatively, it was the voice in his head. He smiled; he was hardly shaking in his boots. If there was a resident ghost, possibly even a troupe of ghostly entertainers, they would have to do better than that if they were going to scare the living daylights out of him. Perhaps these ghostly magicians and conjurers would turn out to be his ticket to fame and fortune. He should befriend the ghosts – they could be his assistants in his magic act, there to help him do magic on and off stage.

Benjamin H. Blackstone, the Greatest Playground Magician in the World – the girls would drool over him and the boys would look up to him; he could tour the schools of the world, become famous like Harry Potter.

Harry Potter was always disappearing from one world into another, poor boy trapped in time, the new Peter Pan of magic, flogged like a dead horse until he could no longer do magic to save his life. But that was the modern world – take an idea, a good or great one, and flog it to death until all the magic was drained out of it. This left the idea like an empty shell or an old magician's trunk, full of nothing but dust, a poor man's Pandora's Box. This was why Benjamin Blackstone wished to disappear back to the past when magic still had the X factor, before the word 'magic' lost its magic.

Benjamin's two heroes of magic, Harry Houdini and Robert-Houdin, had left the stage some time ago. These days, there were so many magicians practising magic on the stage, on the street or on the magical medium of television, Benjamin could not see any room for him on this overcrowded street. The street through Benjamin's eyes did not seem magical in any way shape or form; it certainly wouldn't be considered a magical street like Main Street in New York or Beale Street in Memphis.

In truth, the magical medium of television wasn't as magical as it had been in his grandfather's day, John Logie Baird's magical box of tricks which his grandfather called 'this small magic box'. The television had always been somewhat of a Pandora's Box but these days the magic once contained in the box seemed to have disappeared to be replaced by second-hand, even third-hand magic. Benjamin's grandfather said the magical box of tricks no longer had the power to perform magic; it was like a magic trunk that once upon a time had belonged to one of the great magicians of his grandfather's day, Carter, Blackstone or Thurston. Sadly, like his heroes Houdini and Robert Houdin, those magicians only performed their magic tricks in the spirit world, or so Benjamin's grandfather had told Benjamin with a twinkle in his eyes. Somehow, the magic had been lost to the modern world and once the magic was lost, it was hard to get it back.

Benjamin had always imagined the magic hung in the air like radio waves, air illuminated like fairy sparks before they disappeared into the ether, as if by magic, perhaps exactly like magic, to reappear in another magical space or place. The truth was, some of the old-time radio waves from a time when magical was at its most powerful were still out there in space; any day now, they may be picked up by another world on their transmitters. In another magical world, these transmissions would be marvelled over, treasured as they had been when originally broadcast.

Steam trains were magical and greatly admired by Benjamin; he could easily imagine steam trains on other worlds, perhaps even star steamers steaming their way across the starlit heavens. Perhaps one such star steamer was on its way to earth at this very moment, as Benjamin's imagination began to get up a good head of steam. The boiler in his head was red hot, stoked by the magical space he had just entered as fairy sparks flew out of his eyes and ears as his senses worked overtime to keep up with his imagination. The attic was a world within a world, a most magical place and space, or at least through Benjamin's eyes and imagination, the attic of the mind.

And now Benjamin was standing within spitting distance of the attic, he could hardly contain his excitement; his heart was beating like a big bass drum, but in a good way. The last thing Benjamin Blackstone wanted was to suffer from a rare case of Victorian human spontaneous combustion; if this ever happened this would be dark magic indeed!

Benjamin continued to slowly climb the wooden staircase being careful not to slip, for the wooden staircase was rotten in places. Eventually, after climbing up three flights of stairs (three being the magic number – not if he fell and broke his neck!) he reached the summit, the Holy Grail, the attic. Once again, Benjamin stopped dead in his tracks, not because he was scared of what might be in the attic – after all, attics were often the setting of ghost stories – it was because he was afraid the attic wouldn't live up to the way he had imagined it in his head. Benjamin had built the attic into such unimaginable proportions it was more like a castle or a maharaja's palace than a dusty old attic full of broken toys and tea chests stuffed with old newspaper.

Benjamin nervously reached for the door handle of the attic and as he did so the door slowly creaked as it opened, like in a classic ghost story. The door was now ajar, although not in any magical way – Benjamin just about stopped himself making the old joke – 'When is a door not a door?' – for he was certain it would fall on deaf ears. Benjamin wondered if in fact the attic was encouraging him to have a quick peek inside, crane his head around the door, then the Attic Museum would close its doors for the day. Or so he was thinking as an imaginary man appeared out of thin air doing his job of being a Jobsworth. But before Benjamin could take a peek, the door closed, slamming shut, almost cutting him in half as he tried to enter. It was as if the ghostly magician who lived in the attic was attempting the 'Sawing the Lady in Half' routine, replacing the lady with a young man, more mind magic of a dark variety, as Benjamin's imagination continued to take a walk on the wild side.

'Hey, I didn't get my money's worth!' cried Benjamin as if he just placed a penny into the slot of an old arcade machine called 'What the Butler Saw' at the end of a pier – nothing in this case!

'Not a bad trick!' sniffed Benjamin rather dismissively, clapping his hands together in mock appreciation as if he imagined the attic was a giant magician and he was the small audience of one. This small audience of one was unimpressed, partly due to the fact that even some old magic had lost its magic over the years, so much so it seemed like poor man's magic, party magic, the sort that Benjamin abhorred.

Perhaps the whole house was a stage prop for a giant magician, thought Benjamin, and now he was trapped in the trick as he became the magician's beautiful assistant. Not if he couldn't get out of the trick and was found decades later as a skeleton, his bony fingers half in and half out of the giant magic trunk as if he was trying to use one of his fingers as a skeleton key to unlock the box to escape a fate worse than death. Trouble was, Benjamin Blackstone was no Harry Houdini, the greatest escapologist of them all; he was barely a magician, other than the World's Worst Magician, a title he had bestowed upon himself.

Now that would be quite a story, Benjamin thought. He wasn't a half bad storyteller, he was certainly a far better storyteller than a magician – perhaps this was his gift, where his talents lay? A good storyteller was a bit like a magician or a conjurer – they conjured up the magic onto the written page, they were masters of misdirection, 'prestidigitation', as it was called in the circles magic was practised within. Now you see it, now you don't. *Now you don't in this case*, Benjamin thought, as a wry smile appeared on his face and then disappeared in the blinking of an eye.

Benjamin then stepped back from the door and if this was indeed all a game the spirit magician was playing, then he would buy into it; after all, he had already bought a ticket to the show the moment he stepped into the house. Only time would tell if this was a magical moment or not. Of course, this ticket was as imaginary as a virtual ticket, and virtual magic certainly wasn't Benjamin's cup of tea and nor were the so-called technological wizardry and wonders the virtual world provided. Benjamin was more 'old school' – not surprising considering his family, the Blackstones, were all involved in the magic trade in one way or another.

'Oh well, the show's over, better be off, places to go, people to see; got an appointment with Mr Houdini at two o'clock and Mr Houdin at five o'clock to discuss the possibility of them teaming up as a magic act, putting old rivalries to one side.' If Benjamin wasn't to be a magician, perhaps he could become a manager of magic acts, an impresario, set up his own company, tour the world with the best magicians from all eras, ghostly magicians which included this imaginary magic business, Blackstone Entertainments. The Attic Magician might well be interested to join his company if he ever got an appointment to see him in the flesh! Benjamin raised his voice as he turned on his heels and made for the stairs.

'I'll be off then and I won't be coming back. I'm bored of magic, I think I'll take up stamp collecting instead!'

The door creaked as if it was talking to him, not yapping as in a haunted house, the door opening and slamming time and time again, almost breaking the hinges off the door completely. Eventually, the door would fly off, making a poor magic man's magic carpet, which had more holes in it than the swords in the wardrobe illusion, another old trick which had lost its magic some time ago.

Benjamin turned around, fully expecting the door to be open this time as the magician and attic welcomed him in with open arms, but this was not to be the case. Benjamin could see this wasn't going to be easy, but then again, achieving your dreams, conjuring up your own magic moments, was never going to be easy – his parents and grandparents had taught him that much.

Benjamin decided he would take the bull by the horns so he backed off then rushed at the door, this time expecting it to fly open as he fell into the room like in an old silent comedy starring Buster Keaton or Harold Lloyd. Those old silent films were magical, far more magical than the modern movies or anything on the television these days. The door still did not budge as Benjamin hit the door and fell to the ground like a rag doll. He didn't cry out, he just grunted as he picked himself up and dusted himself down. Benjamin was 100% the dust he was brushing off his old Victorian frock coat was not fairy or magic dust, just dust the sort that made you sneeze.

'Attisshhhhoooo, there are more ways to skin a cat,' Benjamin mumbled under his breath as he bent down and peered through the keyhole, hoping he wasn't met by a giant bloodshot eyeball belonging to a giant, or poked in the eye with a giant magic wand!

'Nothing!' exclaimed Benjamin, describing what he had seen: nothing. Not 'nothing special', simply 'nothing'. The room was pitch black; he couldn't see a thing. Not seeing a thing of course made Benjamin even more curious as to what was in the attic; something special must be in that room otherwise he would have been in and out by now without touching the sides. Benjamin's mind started to work its own kind of magic, the kind of magic all storytellers experienced when a good or great idea popped into their head as if by magic. The things Benjamin's imagination conjured up for him at that moment – a magical one in his mind – would make your toes curl and your hair stand upon end like fairy sparks. And there were fairies in the attic, hundreds of them spinning furiously away upon spinning wheels causing sparks to fly everywhere. Yes, the attic would catch fire, as would the house and he along with it, so all anybody would find in the charred ruins were his ashes, and there was nothing magical about ashes even if they were kept in a magical-looking black tea caddy painted with gold and silver dragons.

Still, the door would not open so in the end Benjamin decided the time was not right for him to be invited into the inner magic circle of the attic; the Attic Magician was testing him. Just how badly did Benjamin Blackstone want to see this Attic Magic? For a magician, timing was everything. The time was not right; he must bide his time. So Benjamin decided to sleep in the old house overnight. He would phone his parents and say he was staying over at a friend's house – a white lie. He had a friend whose parents were away on holiday so he was sure this small piece of stage misdirection would work; yes, the old stage patter of a magician would not let him down, the old silver tongue. Trouble was, with his lack of magical ability, even this small deception was a risk but one he thought well worth taking; even if this deception was discovered, he would simply tell his parents the true story. The story Benjamin the storyteller would make up was a simple one: that he'd spent the night in a haunted house for retired magicians, one of which was his great-grandfather, Atticus Blackstone, the black sheep of the family, end of story. More than likely the end of his not-so-magical story if he was not careful, for his parents would ground him for the rest of his life! It seemed that Benjamin really was from a family of entertainers and magicians, often seen in the public's eyes as overly dramatic and overly theatrical.

Benjamin decided he would give himself the guided tour of the house and hope a ghostly tour guide carrying his own skull under his arm didn't step in and take over. A few hours later, for the house was like a giant maze with hundreds of rooms, Benjamin finally found a room that suited his needs, a large room on the second floor. The dusty old bed chambers had an old-fashioned magical-looking brass bed set in the corner and in the other corner, a cabinet of curiosity. The brass bed was the sort one often sees in period dramas and children's films where some sort of magic is involved – either the bed could fly or it sat on the seabed. The cabinet of curiosity was made of ebony; it was exquisite, a work of art in its own right, but Benjamin's curiosity was piqued, as was he. so he climbed into bed and no sooner had his head hit the pillow than he was sound asleep.

2

Hey Presto!

Surprisingly enough, Benjamin got a good night's sleep; there were no spooks flying above his head waking him from his slumbers and his brass bed didn't take him on a flight of fancy around the house, or the stars, as he swapped an English midsummer's night for an Arabian nightmare! What was a nightmare was sleep-walking, something Benjamin had suffered from since he was a young child; sleep-walking in this death trap of a house was sure to turn into a waking nightmare.

Perhaps the attic would be in a better mood today, for Benjamin was sure the attic was keeping a secret and one that may open up a whole new world for him. Benjamin did not have a crystal ball in his jacket pocket – for one, he was not wearing his magician's stage gear, and nor did he have a crystal ball in his head as some stage magicians appeared to have as they performed their fantastical mind-reading acts on stage. It was again Benjamin's misfortune that this was not the case, for a whole new world was about to open up for Benjamin and one so fantastical he could not have imagined or conjured it from his mind in a million light years. The floorboards did not open up and the house, not being a monster, did not swallow him whole, but something did open up – several things in fact.

As Benjamin walked up the last flight of stairs towards the attic, he pictured a giant – no not a giant but the child of a giant – sitting outside the attic door with something in their hands. The closer he got to the attic, the clearer the picture became – the object was made of paper, a simple illusion worked by the fingers, the paper opened and closed and each time it happened, a number appeared, one which the observer had to pick, which revealed a secret message. Except in this case, the trick revealed a picture in the attic of his mind, which was of him reading a book. There was more to it than that but the image faded as Benjamin found himself outside the door, now wide open, inviting him into this secret circle.

Benjamin stood frozen to the spot, mesmerised, spellbound by the open door, sure that no sooner did he move towards the door of the attic it would slam shut as it had done before. Perhaps this time it would take his hand clean off as if the attic door had now become an old-fashioned rusty kissing gate in the country, dividing one piece of land from another. A one-handed magician was no good to man or beast and if the door cut him in half he may well get a chance to tread the boards in all the haunted houses across the land, perhaps even the world. Had a magician or illusionist ever attempted to cut themselves in half before? If they had, surely the trick must have gone wrong – badly wrong!

Could it be the door of the attic was dividing one world from another? His world, no longer being a magical one, and the one in the attic, being the most magical place in any world, in whatever time frame that was? A framed slide of a magic lantern appeared in Benjamin's mind but there was nothing in it. What did this signify? Probably that, like an old magician's trunk, there was nothing in his head but sawdust!

Scarecrows were often used in old black and white movies to scare the audience half to death; perhaps there was an old scarecrow behind the attic door waiting to scare him to death. Well. why do things by half? A grimace appeared upon Benjamin's face, a twisted smile – more a twitch than anything more sinister. Benjamin was indeed getting twitchy.

'What are you waiting for? I don't bite!' a disembodied voice laughed in manic fashion quite in keeping with a Victorian ghost story, or so Benjamin imagined. For the house, apart from a few creaking floorboards, was as quiet as the proverbial mouse. The truth was, in old houses it wasn't mice you had to worry about, it was rats the size of cats as one scurried out of the attic past Benjamin and ran down the staircase and out of sight as if being chased by a giant cat, a wild cat.

This wasn't a good start; Benjamin was beginning to think the attic belonged to a child named Pandora who had just opened up her magical box/trunk, letting out all manner of horrors into the house. The haunted house, clearly magical in some way, transformed into a house-of-horrors dark magic. Was this a ghost story after all and would Benjamin finish the story as a ghost writer – a dead ghost writer?

'Pull yourself together, Benjamin Blackstone. What happened to your stiff upper lip?' Benjamin grunted under his breath, wishing he hadn't mentioned the word stiff, as in stiffs or corpses. Benjamin straightened his back, straightened his attire and straightened his imaginary magician's top hat as if about to go on stage as he took a big gulp of air, closed his eyes and walked through the door repeating the mantra to himself, 'I must believe, I must believe, I must believe.'

Three was the magic number; the trick worked, deceiving the mind, not an easy trick to pull off. Benjamin was in, as the attic door slowly closed behind him, creaking all the way as if the ghostly magician wanted to give him his money's worth. The more likely story was the ghostly magician wanted to spook him big time. Benjamin wondered if he was 'in', as he put it, or if he was trapped, trapped in a haunted house, and trapped in an attic. What next? Trapped in a magic trunk that suddenly sprang open as he tripped and fell into it never to be seen again?

The wheel of fortune turned once more and this time for the better as the sun appeared outside the small round attic window and the attic was flooded with light, a simple illusion performed by Mother Nature, the only great female magician and one who performed her illusions and tricks of the light in a giant magic circle that encompassed the earth.

'I knew it, I knew the attic would reveal its secrets, its magic, its tricks to a fellow magician, and what magic!' cried Benjamin in wonder and amazement. But what exactly was he seeing? Was he seeing what he thought he was seeing or was this another illusion, a trick of the mind? Was he seeing what he wanted to see, what he wished to believe more than anything? That Attic Magic was a fact and not a far-fetched fiction that writers conjured up from the magic in their heads.

Perhaps there really was nothing in the attic, nothing in the giant's magic trunk or magic carpet bag, a bag that once upon an Arabian time was a magic carpet belonging to one of Ali Baba's forty thieves. There was nothing in this dusty attic but dust and it wasn't magic, fairy, gold or moon dust, certainly not stardust unless there was a hole in the roof. This dust was simply the sort of dust that made one sneeze!

'Haaaaaaatishooooooo!' Benjamin sneezed again for the second time since he'd entered the house, causing even more dust to circulate in the attic. 'Haaaaaatishoooo, Hatishooo!'

Three definitely wasn't the magic number in this case. Benjamin opened his eyes and saw nothing; there wasn't anything in the attic, nothing at all – well, apart from dust. Unless of course the attic had a secret compartment like all good and bad magician's magic trunks. Perhaps there were untold treasures in the attic covered in a cloak of invisibility, a cloak belonging to a giant magician? Benjamin rubbed the sleep and the dust out of his eyes; if he waited long enough the magic would come, it had to. The magic would not come if a person wanted it to come; desperation was dark magic, magic didn't work like that, magic was an organic process, it could not be forced or conjured as in simple stage magic. In fact, you couldn't stage natural magic, it was a law unto itself. So Benjamin decided to play it cool as he sat cross-legged on the floorboards and shut his eyes as if sitting upon a magic carpet in a palace in Persia.

Alternatively, Benjamin was a Buddhist monk high in the mountains, meditating. He could wait for the magic – unlike the modern child, he had patience, he had all the time in the world. After all, he was in a magical space, a magical place, and as such, a magic circle surrounded him, surrounded the attic. Perhaps it surrounded the house, too, especially as the house was situated in the country, an old hamlet trapped in time, trapped within a magic circle.

Time seemed to stand still as Benjamin entered a trance-like state.

Then Benjamin heard a rustling sound, at first no louder than a mouse. As, by this time, Benjamin was in a deep state of meditation, he did not appear to hear the sound. Then as the seconds flew by, the rustling grew into a knocking sound and then a rapping noise, which grew louder and louder.

Immediately, Benjamin opened his eyes like the shutters of an old Edwardian camera; he couldn't see for the life of him anything which would cause the knocking sound. The sound was emanating from… no, not from the wall, but behind the wall, causing Benjamin to imagine a giant rat scurrying around behind the wall. Benjamin jumped to his feet like a jack out of a jack-in-a-box and walked towards the wall in jerky fashion like an old clockwork tin soldier. Benjamin stopped in an abrupt manner as if the key in his back needed winding up, then he bent down and pressed his ear against the wall. The sound of knocking came again as if someone was banging on the wall, not an animal but a person. Had someone been walled up in a small secret room? If so, perhaps this was their ghost wanting to be let out?

Benjamin ran his hand across the rough wooden wall several times. He could feel something, almost as if there was a small door covered up by the old peeling wallpaper. He tore at the wallpaper, furiously tearing it off, causing two of his nails to break, until much to his surprise and amazement, a small white wooden door appeared.

'Hey presto!' Benjamin cheered in triumph. 'You see, all attics are magical; there isn't a single attic in the whole wide world that does not have the ability to conjure up something magical of one kind or another.' Benjamin stopped, his heart in his mouth, half wanting to open the door, half not, as if he was now imagining there was a large rat on the other side of the door, perhaps an entire family of rats, giant rats. Did he really want giant rats in the same room as he was, scurrying about under his feet chewing whatever they could find, namely Benjamin H. Blackstone!?

What if the door was locked and needed a key? Yes, that must be it, it was far too easy for the door just to open… sesame!

'Hey presto!' exclaimed Benjamin, as no sooner had he reached for the small doorknob than it sprang open to reveal a magic trunk with stickers all over it from countries all across Europe. Was this magic trunk his great-grandfather's magic trunk – Atticus Blackstone, the black sheep of the Blackstone family – and if so, why was it hidden away in the secret cupboard in the attic?

Benjamin held his breath as he opened the trunk for it was not locked. Once again, Benjamin was disappointed, for there was nothing in the trunk. Benjamin had a thought: most magic trunks had a false bottom; perhaps that was why the trunk was not locked? Benjamin felt all around the bottom of the box as his excitement reached fever pitch, and just when he thought his luck was out, the bottom of the trunk sprang open as if it was the top of the trunk. Out popped a book, a Victorian popup book. 'Hey presto!' Benjamin could not help himself exclaiming for the second time in as many moments –unquestionably a magic moment this time round. The old book was entitled *Abracadabra Street*.

'Unbelievable! The story's true, the one my parents told me about my great-grandfather Atticus and a magical book from the Victorian era!' cried Benjamin, finishing off his sentence as if it had been one written for him many, many moons ago.

Benjamin stared wildly at the book, his eyes almost popping out of his head. He was spellbound, entranced, amazed, astounded, as all the magic words flew out of his head at once. He was not sure if this extraordinary happening, a magical one, was real or simply a conjuration of the mind as the magician in his head worked his dark magic. When the mind worked, it worked like magic, and when it did not, the magic it conjured up was indeed a dark magic, or so he recalled his father telling him one day. This day had been a dark one, a day when his father was obviously in a dark place, a place that was anything but magical. Why was this happening to him of all people, Benjamin Blackstone, a boy who couldn't do magic to save his life? In his mind, Benjamin was the World's Worst Magician, a title he had bestowed upon himself having failed to deliver the magic on or off stage.

Benjamin's father often disappeared into a dark world of his own when his moods became blacker than the Black Hole of Calcutta; these were dark days indeed. Benjamin imagined on these dark days his father would climb into the magic trunk in his head to escape the world. His father had surrounding himself with a dark magic circle which stopped anyone entering his magical space. In actuality, in the real world, his father's escape, his magic trunk, his magical space, was the shed at the bottom of the garden. Here his father locked himself away until he had finished building his latest illusion; once his father had shut the door of the shed and locked the door behind him, Benjamin and his mother wouldn't see him for days, sometimes not for weeks. That was until he appeared, as if by magic, all smiles, with a trick or illusion he imagined would dazzle, amaze and astound the world of magic. Now sometimes his father's magic tricks did dazzle, amaze and astound the magic world and sometimes they did not. When the magic did not work, his father appeared to imagine dark magical forces were at work, ones hell-bent on stopping him from working his magic. It was these times that Benjamin's father did not work, metaphorically speaking and in the real sense of the word, to work, as in earning a living.

'Can you really work magic? That's hard to believe; by the moth-eaten appearance of the book, I'm beginning to think you're nothing more than a piece of Victorian memorabilia,' grunted Benjamin, once again talking to himself, for he was more than a little surprised to find the book had no writing in it, no story, unless it was written in invisible ink. Furthermore, there appeared to be only one double-page of a street lined with shops on both sides; perhaps it was the sort of book for young children to play make-believe with, a street you could carry around with you wherever you went. It was up to the reader to make up the story from the objects on the street, or perhaps like a magician's magic trunk, it too had a false bottom, perhaps like a magic dot-to-dot book – if you stared at it long enough, the image on the page would change before your very eyes, exactly by magic.

Benjamin sat patiently waiting for the show to begin, but once again nothing happened. Benjamin was about to turn his back and walk away, hoping the street theatre that he felt should be entertaining him would only happen if he pretended he was no longer interested. The street magicians had overdone the old suspense, losing their small audience of one. Still, nothing happened. Was he missing something? Of course he was missing something; he was missing the magic, or moreover, the magic word was missing: abracadabra. So Benjamin delivered the most overused word in magic circles, apart from the word magic itself, and did it in such a flowery way, one could easily have imagined he was delivering the line to princes, maharajas, kings, queens and emperors who had come halfway across the world to see him perform at the famed Attic Magic Club: 'A-b-r-a-c-a-d-a-b-r-a!'

Still nothing. How bad a magician could he be? He was performing magic in an attic, the most magical place and space there was, and still he couldn't perform magic.

'Take a bow, Benjamin Blackstone – the World's Worst Magician!' a disembodied voice cried in a theatrical manner, as all Benjamin could hear was boos ringing in his ears, though in truth it could have been his tinnitus playing tricks on him, as it often did in times of stress.

It looked for all the world that Benjamin Blackstone's magical story had ended before it had begun, dark magic indeed, no doubt of the quantum variety.

3

The Magic Word

Another idea sprang into his fevered mind – what if he said the word three times? A magic mantra after all – three was supposed to be the magic number. So Benjamin tried again, putting his heart and soul into the delivery of this most magical of words, 'Abracadabra, abracadabra, a...' Before he had a chance to finish the magic mantra, something finally began to happen, something amazing, astounding, unbelievable, as the book began to move in his hand. He then heard voices, hundreds of tiny voices, ones he imagined were coming out of the book itself, unless a crowd of spirits had gathered around him in a dark magic circle all eager to see the show.

'This cannot be happening!' exclaimed Benjamin under his breath. It simply could not be, the whole thing must be down to his vivid imagination. It was either that or he had fallen asleep on the floor of the attic and this was just a surreal dream. He hadn't even finished the magic mantra; perhaps he was getting the hang of this magic lark or perhaps, in his excitement, he had forgotten he had uttered the magic word three times. As they often say in magic circles, once the Jinn is out of the bottle, you can't put it back in, or in this case, the magic word back into the mouth of the magician.

There: he had said it. He was a magician, albeit with the help of a magic book and a magical space, that of an old attic – attic magic was at work. Alternatively, and there was always an alternative in life and in acts of magic, including the magic of life and the universe and alternate realties, this had nothing to do with the attic, which meant the Victorian popup book had taken centre stage, using the attic to stage this fantastical feat of extraordinary magic.

The feat of fantastical extraordinary magic hadn't happened yet unless Benjamin Blackstone had a crystal ball in his head. Could it be the movement of the book was simply a bad sleight-of-hand trick, for it was true that, ever since he had entered the attic, he had been as nervous as a kitten, like a black cat on a hot tin roof. Yes, that was it, his hands had gone into a spasm as sometimes happened to nervous magicians when they stepped upon a stage for the first, and sometimes last, time: stage fright. Benjamin was sure Sherlock Holmes would agree with him although the man pulling the detective's strings, the science-minded Sir Arthur Conan Doyle, a man who believed in the spirit world and had tried to put it under a microscope, may not. He may have believed this was indeed down to powerful spirits, for the spirit world was all around us, an unseen world, a kind of magic, albeit a dark and barely understood one.

Benjamin's eyes were glued to the book although thankfully not literally for, as yet, a mischievous poltergeist had not come out to play dirty tricks upon the boy.

'Come on, come on,' Benjamin grunted, almost willing the book to conjure up some magic, any magic, even small-time magic would do.

The book appeared to be listening for it flew open, causing magic dust to fly everywhere, or so Benjamin was now thinking, and Victorian magic dust at that, and if this was true he was also breathing in Victorian air, as Benjamin imagined the book as a time capsule. Benjamin then dropped the book like a hot potato onto the floor of the attic as if suddenly it had turned red hot – clearly dark magic at work.

'What on earth?' exclaimed Benjamin as the book appeared to grow before his very startled amazed and wild eyes. He then picked himself up off the floor and walked towards the book now the size of a children's playhouse, probably one belonging to a child named Pandora. Benjamin looked exactly as if he'd seen a ghost, several in fact. By this time, the popup book was ten times its size, so much so that Benjamin had to stand on tiptoes to see into the book.

The cacophony of voices grew ever louder so it sounded to him as if the excited voices were all bartering in a bazaar in some foreign magical land. An attic was a foreign land, a most magical foreign land, a cross between Arabia, Timbuktu and Constantinople, plus all the magical story lands ever imagined up from the minds of the gifted storytellers, who'd conjured these lands out of their heads by magic, the magic of the mind.

Benjamin grasped hold of the cover of the book for dear life because by now the old popup book was beginning to slowly close. Before he knew it, Benjamin was swinging from the top of the cover of the book like an acrobat who had fallen off a high wire. As he looked down, he saw that the book was now covering half the attic space, and if he let go he felt sure he would break something – no doubt the humerus, the funny bone. So Benjamin clambered up a little higher so he could take a peek inside the book.

'Hey presto!' exclaimed Benjamin uttering a magic word, for this seemed the appropriate response for a magician to cry when something magical happened, almost as if it had happened out of thin air. Benjamin could not think of a better word in the circumstances, for what he saw amazed, astounded and delighted him. There was a street and on both sides of the street, shops and most if not all of the shops appeared to be magic shops. Outside the shops stood magicians, street magicians, all trying to outdo the other magicians on the street – Abracadabra Street – and over there on the corner of the street was Davenport's Magic, the oldest magic shop in the world and it sat on another magical street, one paved not with yellow brick but with gold, for you see this street was in London. Now that was no wonder tale, or moreover a tale about Dick Whittington and his cat, no doubt a black cat that could perform black magic at the drop of a wizard's hat!

There were even magicians performing tricks in the shop window, one clearly in the middle of performing card tricks to the people on the other side of the glass. Clearly, the window of the shop was a magical looking glass for the magician leaned forward and held out his arm, which easily passed through the glass. An open-mouthed member of the audience standing outside the shop took the card, looked at it behind his hand then placed it back into the pack of cards, as the magician took the card and pulled his hand back through the glass. Benjamin was fully expecting the glass window to crack and the magician's hand be cut to ribbons, but this was not the case.

'Small-time magic is what I asked for and small-time magic I got, except this isn't small-time magic, this is big-time magic!' cried Benjamin, the words tumbling out of his mouth like the stage patter of a magician going on stage for the first time. The adrenalin was rushing around his body so fast, which meant he was rushing his delivery. Some magician said their first time on stage seemed to drag on forever; those waiting in the wings said for them the act appeared to fly by as the magician performed his magic in something of a whirlwind fashion. For the audience's part, their heads were in a spin turning first left, then right, then left again, as the magician paced and sometimes raced from one side of the stage in a manic state of high agitation.

Benjamin watched the little magician in the shop window shuffle the pack before the man's card, the Ace of Spades, rose out of the pack and floated through the letter box in the door of the shop and into the air, disappearing like a tiny magic carpet. 'Now if you'd like to check your inside pocket,' the magician said, looking at the man who had taken the card. The man duly obliged, holding up the Ace of Spades. The magician in the shop window took a bow as the audience outside the shop, who had been open-mouthed a few seconds earlier, broke into wild applause. In the blink of an eye, the magic shop, which was half empty, soon became buzzing, full to the brim with people buying magic tricks, books, illusion and the like. Benjamin had never seen the like in his life before, real magic! He was so excited that, in his excitement to get a closer look and get closer to the action, he fell off his position perched on the top of the cover of the book.

The next thing he knew he was lying on the ground looking up at the rafters in the attic. A few seconds after that, everything went dark as the book slammed shut. Benjamin was trapped; still, nothing to worry about, after all he was trapped in his old life, trapped in a haunted house, trapped in an attic. So therefore, being trapped in a book was nothing to write home about, apart from the little fact that this book was clearly a magical book, possibly one possessed by the spirit of a dead magician. The magician in question could, at a pinch of magic dust, even be his great-grandfather, the black sheep of the Blackstone family, steeped in magic since the dawn of time.

4

Abracadabra Street

'What on earth are you doing down there, boy?' laughed a man with a large pack of cards in his hands. He was shuffling the pack with one hand, quite a neat trick, or so Benjamin thought, trying to get his bearings. 'No, don't tell, me the cards will tell me when they're ready,' the man said, looking at the cards in his hands: Tarot cards. One card rose to the top of the pack, a simple-enough trick for a skilled close-up magician, although one Benjamin had never been able to perfect without half the cards ending up on the floor. 'It's your good fortune, my boy, that you've met me and not some of the more, shall we say, shady magicians on the street,' the magician said, brandishing a Tarot card with an illustration of a wheel of fortune on it.

'I was listening,' Benjamin replied, making up a tale on

the spot, and Benjamin had always been good at making up magical tales.

'Magic, yes, if you were listening to the street, which I can well imagine to be true street magic, the magic of the street. I can see you're in tune with magic. Not sure if you're in tune with the street, though?' grunted the man, looking a might puzzled at this strange boy, for to the man he seemed somehow out of place and possibly out of time as well.

Benjamin wondered if the man was performing a trick – after all, he had all the old patter – as smooth as silk, the words tumbled out of his mouth. However, Benjamin didn't quite mean it as a compliment, for by 'trick', he meant a scam, a dirty trick. How often had the magician performed this trick? More times than Benjamin had had hot dinners – the whole pack of Tarot cards were probably the same; they probably all had a depiction of a wheel of fortune on them. The man smiled but it seemed like a crooked sort of smile to Benjamin. Of course, that might be the man's misfortune; he might have been born that way. 'You should never judge a book by its cover,' – Benjamin heard the voice of his father in his head. His father, mother and his grandparents and his home in suburbia seemed as far away as if on another planet at this moment in time.

Was this moment to be a magical moment, one that stretched as far as the imagination of a child? Or would it be a moment that Benjamin would wish had never happened? It was at that moment that a man passed by pushing a barrel organ and on the organ was a monkey, and one performing magic, believe it or not, a card trick. The pack of cards were normal size and the sleight-of-hand magic shuffling of the pack by the monkey was astounding. Benjamin felt as if the monkey was making a monkey out of him, for the truth was that the monkey was a better magician than he imagined he'd ever be.

So this wasn't to be that magic moment, at least not yet; the street, like a magician, was keeping him in suspense, stretching it out as long as it could so a moment felt like a day, a week or, heaven forbid, a whole year. Benjamin was impatient; he wanted to be a great magician yesterday, as the modern expression went, but these were the times of the Victorian – both light and dark magic, and everything went at a more sedate pace, just like living in the country.

'You can't put the Jinn back in the bottle once you've let him out.' This time, the voice in his head was that of his grandfather who was no longer in this world as he had passed the previous year. Perhaps his great-grandfather was now in the spirit world performing his magic tricks and illusions; perhaps this was the spirit world, in which case if he walked on down the street he might well bump into his grandfather; perhaps, at a pinch of magic dust, his great-grandfather.

Benjamin wondered if his grandfather was the one who had created this illusion, this magic trick, in other words if he had built the giant popup book with his own hands. By that, Benjamin wasn't being metaphorical, he really meant he had built the trick, as his father had built tricks in his workshop, the garden shed. Perhaps his grandfather had not been able to follow the light, the beam of a giant magic lantern, as Benjamin imagined the light leading to heaven. Trapped on earth, for he felt he had unfinished business, wanting to make up for the dirty tricks he had played upon his own family, he had become the Shadow Conjurer, the puppet master, and all the characters in the book entitled *Abracadabra Street* were his puppets. Was he still talking in the metaphorical sense or was he simply talking nonsense? Was magic really possible, unseen magic, dark magic that nobody, even the most brilliant of minds, could truly understand?

The world and the universe was full of magic; it was truly a weird and wonderful place, weirder and more wonderful than the human mind could possibly imagine, beyond the imagination. There was no such place beyond the imagination and if there was, as soon as you stepped into that space and out of it again, like a magic wardrobe or a dark looking glass, you forgot all you had seen there; it was a Catch-22.

Benjamin felt electricity pulsating under his feet, entering his legs, then his body, until it reached his mind. His eyes lit up like the beam of a magic lantern as he stood bolt upright, as if the surge of electricity this magical street had given him had done the trick. Or perhaps it was the Victorian magic dust he had breathed in when the book had first opened, as if the book was a magic shop that had been closed for hundreds of years and was now reopening its door for business once more. Benjamin was walking on air, illuminated air in this case; he felt more alive than he ever had in his world. He was sure on this street he would be able to perform magic – his wish had come true. But was this down to the magical Victorian popup book named *Abracadabra Street*, or was it down to the magical attic, attic magic, as he called it?

The cardboard cut-out characters that had been standing frozen to the spot were now moving about freely, made of flesh and blood as real as Benjamin Blackstone, as real as anybody he had ever met. Once again, Benjamin had to pinch himself, for he could not be sure how real this street was; it could fold up at any moment and he'd be crushed to death. For a second, Benjamin wanted to climb up the shopfront of one of the magic shops in his attempt to escape this world, but then thought better of it as the magic shop might well collapse and he'd be crushed underneath it.

'Hold on a minute – the shops are made of cardboard, as is the street, as is the book. Magic? Don't make me laugh, it is no more magical than the one-dimensional paper-cut figures in a children's storybook for under-fives,' huffed Benjamin, sounding older than his years.

However, Benjamin soon came to the few senses God gave him, for he really did not think this was the case. There was a story here, half true, half made-up, a story he needed to follow if he was ever to see the light of day again. Could the same be said of his great-grandfather, Atticus Blackstone, if he too were trapped in this unreal world? Only time would tell.

Benjamin needed to follow the story and follow the magic, for like the other characters on the street, ones that at first appeared as shadowy, one-dimensional paper-cut figures, he was now a part of the story set on a magical street. If this story was to work like clockwork then he must believe; belief was the key to everything, the world around him and the universe itself only worked if you believed it did.

Then a thought occurred to him: as there only appeared to be one page in the book, wouldn't everything get old very quickly, as the modern expression went? Well it was an old book but living in the modern age of new technological wizardry had, to Benjamin's mind, being an old-school sort of boy, got old very quickly indeed. Another left-field thought came quick on the heels of the last one as if he was being chased across Abracadabra Street by the infamous Victorian villain Spring-Heeled Jack. Did the page of the book change while your back was turned or did it change while you were looking at it like a magic 3-d dot-to-dot book?

By the looks of it, Abracadabra Street was the most magical street in the world for this street truly was a world street. Benjamin imagined that all the best magicians and conjurers of all time lived and worked on this street. The magic was certainly working its magic on him and he hoped it would rub off on him so he too could perform great feats of magic. As Benjamin walked down the streets with the jaunty air of a dandy without a care in the world (or at least not in this unreal world), his eyes were as wide as saucers. Perhaps eyes on stalks would be a more apt description, or perhaps adding the two descriptions together – saucers spinning upon poles, an old trick that music-hall entertainers performed in Vaudeville.

That was funny, he was sure Davenport's Magic, a shop the Blackstone family had frequented more times than he'd had hot dinners, had moved – as it had moved in the real world when it closed down in 2020 while looking for a new site in central London. When Benjamin had first seen the shop it was at one end of the street, yet now the shop was situated in the middle of the street. Mind you, at the time he had first seen the street, he had been hanging off the top of a giant Victorian popup book as his life flashed before him at great speed.

Benjamin had another imagining as he envisaged Davenport's Magic as a giant playing card being shuffled by the King of the Cards and one of his magic heroes, Robert Houdin. As the shops were all made of cardboard, little more than facades, as was the street, then this was hardly surprising. At this moment in time, Davenport's Magic Shop only stood on Abracadabra Street, but one day Benjamin was sure it would pop up again on a street in London exactly by magic, for it was such a magical shop. Benjamin imagined a ghostly outline of where the shop had stood in the London Underground arcade in Strand station, with all the ghosts of the past magicians, conjurers and makers of magic tricks still frequenting, unaware the shop had disappeared off the magic map. Except it had not, for it had popped up as if by magic on Abracadabra Street; if that wasn't magic, nothing was possibly quantum magic, but nevertheless magic all the same. People imagined that quantum magic was a new thing; not so – it had been around since the early Edwardian times thanks to Albert Einstein, Nils Bohr and Edwin Schrödinger. All of these men were magicians of a sort, ones who could conjure up magical ideas from their heads on the unseen things behind the giant magic curtain by the magic of the mind.

Of course, Davenport's Magic was such a magical shop that even in his world it could move from place to place, from one time to another, exactly like magic. Could one object be in two different places at the same time? According to quantum magic, they could; in fact, an object could be in a thousand and one places at the same time. If this was the case, no doubt Davenport's Magic shop was now doing business on a magical street in Constantinople, Marrakesh and Timbuktu, competing with magic carpet shops and easily holding its own.

Benjamin looked down and was astounded to see his feet were a few inches off the ground. 'The street doesn't fly, does it? It being magical and all,' stuttered Benjamin as he looked down not at his feet but at the street, sure he saw it move.

'It's a magical street, boy, anything's possible. I dare say if all the magicians put their collective minds to it, somehow they could make Abracadabra Street fly. Think of that, we could take our magic shops anywhere in the world; it would save those in the magic trade a whole lot of shoe leather. Trouble is, I haven't got a great head for heights so I'm happy to do my magic right here on earth,' added the man, looking towards the clouds.

'Just how long is this street?' enquired Benjamin, feeling very grown up all of a sudden and, after all, travel broadened the mind. The fact he had never travelled outside London before he went in search of his great-grandfather's mansion was neither here nor there to Benjamin Blackstone, for he had travelled far and wide. In his imagination, he had met kings, and queens, maharajas and princes on his travels, travels that had broadened his mind to the point he felt there wasn't any place in the world that he did not have some knowledge of. It was said, before you put pen to paper, that before becoming a writer of fiction you must travel, experience life, then write your story, for it would make it far more believable.

'How long do you imagine it is?' the man replied, fudging the question because Benjamin imagined even he did not know.

'I imagine it's...' Benjamin started to say as the steam wheels of his imagination began to get up a good head of steam, trying to work out just how long the street was.

'Here, boy, see for yourself,' the man grunted, producing a pair of opera glasses out of a cream-coloured top hat, or so it appeared to Benjamin.

'Th... thank you,' replied Benjamin, more squinting through the opera glasses than gazing, as he felt as if he was peering into a crystal ball made of glazed crystal, for he still could not see the end of the street. In fact, the last shop looked more like a pinprick, the dot over the letter "i" in the word "magic", another fiction to add to all the others that Benjamin's imagination had conjured up for his pleasure and delight. 'It's a long street this Abracadabra Street.'

'I imagine it is, the street being a magical street; in fact, I imagine it's the longest street anywhere in the world,' the man replied, trying hard not to smile, for he himself was not sure if he had told the boy a fact or a fiction or a fairy tale. It was probably a combination of all three, a white lie, and if it snowed, as snow was indeed a most magical substance, then the street would become a giant white magic carpet.

'It's snowing!' Benjamin exclaimed, catching snowflakes in his hand to add to his imaginary snowflake collection, the ones he kept on the shelf in the attic of the mind.

'No imagination required this time round,' the man laughed, once again showing his crooked teeth and for a split-second Benjamin wondered if this man had conjured the snow up, unless this was fake snow, the sort used in movies and television period dramas set in Victorian London. It always seemed to snow in Victorian London. Benjamin didn't think he would like to have lived in Victorian London; it was a bit like living in the Arctic Circle. This giant white circle made up of snow and ice wasn't anywhere near as magical as the Magic Circle in London, or at least not to a boy who liked his creature comforts. Benjamin wondered if he was too soft for this Victorian world, being one of the so-called Snowflake Generation. Then a broad smile appeared on his face, for this world was as fake as fake snow – it was made of cardboard, albeit Victorian cardboard, for that was when the Victorian popup book entitled Abracadabra Street was first published.

Perhaps Abracadabra Street had side streets named Abracadabra Road, Lane, Close, Gardens, etc., etc., and if this street was as long as Benjamin imagined it to be then he was sure there was a lot of etcetera, etcetera regarding this magical street. Of course, as the street was clearly a magical one, the street itself may well have the ability to transform itself, say, into a giant magic ring road, a giant magic circle. Perhaps even into a Mobius strip, a most magical illusion conjured by the German mathematician Mobius.

For a split-second, which seemed like a lifetime to Benjamin, everything appeared to stop, frozen in time, Victorian time, as the whole street returned to its original form – a Victorian popup book made of cardboard. Benjamin tried to distract himself, turning to magic of the mind, prestidigitation, as he tried to imagine this magical street perched on a cloud, and not just a cloud in the sky but a cloud in the heavens, a star cloud. Yes, Abracadabra Street would be right at home on a star cloud. This was wishful thinking on his part on a grand scale. Then a smile appeared on his face, for it seemed to Benjamin Blackstone that wishful thinking on this magical street, this magical world, had already gone right off the scale, into the stratosphere. Yes, it was now snowing on Abracadabra Street, or was that stardust? There must be a gaping hole in the roof of the attic and the Victorian popup book must have popped open! Once again, Sherlock Holmes, the master detective and it appeared magician, for to some he appeared and disappeared exactly like magic, had solved the case, a most magical case, like an old magic trunk in an attic full of magic dust.

Benjamin then had another thought, for stars were suns, huge balls of fire; then his thoughts turned to the tale of Icarus who donned a pair of wings made of feathers and wax, flew too close to the sun then fell to earth to his death. A ride on a magic carpet through the heavens might be a fantastical ride but eventually the magic carpet would catch fire and you would suffer the same fate as poor old Icarus. What on earth was he babbling on about? He was talking nonsense; the stars were painted gold, the heavens painted black and he was trapped in a book inside an attic. The rest was his imagination running wild, trying to stop the claustrophobia he had suffered from ever since he was locked in a magic trunk for a joke by his schoolmates, who then promptly forgot about him. Thankfully, his parents came home from work, heard the banging in the garden shed where his father was working on the trick, and saved him from suffocating.

The trick to magic, his grandfather had once told him, was to believe that, if one believed hard enough, the magic would come; it would turn the ordinary into the extraordinary by the power of the mind. One had to have a strong mind; that way, the illusion would last as long as you wanted, or at least long enough, like a child stretching the imagination at playtime to enjoy the magical moment, one trapped in a magic lantern slide. That was until their mother called them for tea, which broke the spell and returned them to the real world. Suspending one's disbelief was the oldest trick in the storyteller's book, but it was one the reader had to buy into, for without it there was no story.

Benjamin closed his eyes and waited for the magic to sweep him up and whisk him away, waiting for this small world to come alive once again so he too could conjure the magic from his head.

5

The Tarot Card Conjurer

'I wouldn't worry, lad, you're probably standing on an invisible magic carpet,' the old man smiled, revealing a set of crooked teeth, which once again made Benjamin wonder if the man was telling him the truth or a white lie or a flat-out lie. If the carpet of air underneath his feet vanished, he may well find himself flat on his face, as the old man turned bad in front of his very startled eyes, pulling the rug from underneath his feet.

Of course, if this rug wasn't a rug but, by the power of magic, turned out to be a magic carpet, he would soon be back on his feet again before he knew it. Yes, you couldn't sweep someone's dreams under the carpet quite so easily if that carpet was a magic carpet. If this old man practised black magic his intention may be to bring everybody down to his level – street level. Not if Benjamin could do anything about it. Perhaps this was wishful thinking on his part, but being a part of the Blackstone family, steeped in magic, perhaps not in his world, Benjamin felt like a bit-part player in his own life. Here, he felt sure he would take the role of the leading man, or at least leading boy, the starring role. At least he would be a major player on this magical stage both on and off the street, the street life parade. Benjamin felt as if these characters were parading before him as if trying to get a part in this street magic production, which meant he was the director.

Benjamin's teachers had once told his parents at a teachers-parents meeting at school that Benjamin found it difficult to live in the real world; it was almost as if he imagined he was living inside a giant book. If he went into a shop and it wasn't magical enough for him, he would dress the shop up and that went for the shop assistant, turning them from a young man into a wizened antiquarian figure in hat and tails using a magic wand to point out to customers the most magical items on the shelves.

A man appeared to be reading Benjamin's mind, for he appeared within spitting distance of him as if by magic. 'Sorry about that, didn't see you there,' the man coughed, bowing as if on stage as he performed the magic ring trick, also known as the miracle rings. As this rate it would be a miracle if he ever got to take to the stage on Abracadabra Street, as all these magicians and conjurers appeared before his startled eyes by anything but magic, unless it was black or dark magic!

Benjamin thought this trick – appearing out of the street itself – was quite impressive, yes the magician should get a role in his little production, Abracadabra Street. That was until Benjamin twigged as to how the illusion trick was done, for clearly there was a small lift underneath the street, a trapdoor, as often used in stage magic or as he had seen in movies in Main St, New York.

Benjamin had an idea for a great trick – he would make the whole of the street disappear – 'now you see Abracadabra Street, now you don't' – as the street lay down flat as the popup book was closed. Trouble was, that would end the story. Did Benjamin really want to end the story before it had even really begun? At first he would have been glad if this had happened but not now; he was hooked, spellbound, under the spell of this magical street, the magical book and the magical attic, three being the magic number. All of these three magical things all working together to make the magic work – many old-school magicians like Robert Houdin had three parts to their act, each part getting more and more magical until the last part sent the audience into raptures.

6

A Wizard in Name Only

Benjamin really did feel as if he was walking on air; he was sure he would soon be able to perform magic in this world, real magic, when in his world he hadn't even been able to do cheap tricks, party magic; that's if the Conjurer of Tarot Cards kept his Grim Reaper's Card in his pocket for the foreseeable future.

'It's hard to keep your feet on the ground when you're on Abracadabra Street,' the Tarot Card Magician laughed, jumping onto a magic carpet flown by a magic carpet salesman who was delivering a pile of carpets, all magical naturally, to the magic carpet shop at the end of Abracadabra Street. 'I'll see you when I see you, although if I see you before I see you, give me fair warning; my eyes aren't what they used to be. At times, it's like looking through a kaleidoscope, and we all know they can't be relied upon to tell us the truth.'

'What is your name?' cried Benjamin, afraid he would not see the man again or perhaps afraid he would; good or bad, this man was the only friend he had in the entire world. Even if that world was an unreal world, one that may not even exist in the true sense of the word 'real' or 'exist' – but what was real? According to the men in white coats, we couldn't trust our own senses. Like the world about us, our eyes were constantly playing tricks upon us, just like magicians and conjurers, 'Magic Men' in fact, or was that fiction? The lines between fact and fiction were so blurred it was as if we were all looking through a crystal vase made of smoked glass. Even Nostradamus would have had trouble seeing the future if he was living on earth at this moment in time, a time when even the word 'magic' appeared to have lost its magic, its shine. Yes, that was the world all over, all smoke and mirrors, black mirrors without a looking glass in sight.

Benjamin wondered if this man of magic, a master of the art, was the sort of man who preferred to be called 'Maestro', like some great opera singer.

'Wizenbaum!' the man cried out, his voice little more than a whisper as it reached Benjamin's ear.

'You're a wizard!' exclaimed Benjamin, who should have guessed, for the man looked like a wizard, wizened as he was, as thin and crooked as a crooked wand belonging to a giant magician or an ogre, dark magic indeed!

'Wash your mouth out with carbolic soap, boy, I'm not a wizard, I'm a magician, and there's no finer around these parts. Wizard, my bloodshot eye, a wizard in my book of magic is a dirty word – oh, and wash your ears out while you're at it. I said, my name's Wizenbaum, W-i-z-e-n-b-a-u-m!' the man retorted as he reappeared, the sounds of his magic carpet swishing over Benjamin's head, forcing him to duck. That was odd – in the real world you would hear the sound of whatever object was coming towards you, a van, a car or in this instance a magic carpet, before it arrived. Benjamin found himself wondering if everything worked the other way round in this upside down, topsy-turvy world.

'Sorry Mr Wizenbaum,' Benjamin replied more than a little sheepishly, so much so, he hoped this sheep didn't follow him into the magic shop, as in his mind's eye he pictured Alice in a boat, one being rowed by a sheep dressed as an old woman. If this was Wonderland, it certainly was more weird than wonderful – a magical wonderland, small on the outside, large on the inside. That was Davenport's Magic shop in London before it disappeared into thin air, for there was everything a magician could want in that magical shop, even a wizard or a witch would be welcome in that magical shop. Benjamin had to smile, for as he looked up, Davenport's Magic Emporium popped up in front of his eyes on Abracadabra Street. It seemed the shop had been given something of a makeover. Benjamin hoped this didn't take the shine off the shop, removing some of its magic in this magical transformation moving from one world to another.

'One more slip of the tongue like that and you may well be sorry!' grunted the man as this time Mr Wizenbaum whizzed through an open window on the second floor of a shop named Wizenbaum's Magic Emporium. The man disappeared through a window which Benjamin was now imagining as a giant magic Christmas calendar with doors which were opened up on the twelve days leading up to the most magical day of the year, Christmas Day. Each door revealed an old poster of a magician of the old school, who Benjamin had imagined came to life when the door of the advent calendar was opened. The magicians then each did their act for the public who no doubt were waiting outside on the street as the windows of the magician's shop on the second floor were thrown open, Carter, Blackstone,

Houdin (King of Conjurers), Houdini, Thurston, Fra Diavolo (the Great Magician), Servais Le Roy (World's Monarch of Magic), Mr Maskelyne's Sensational Magical Romance – the Philosopher's Stone, way before Harry Potter appeared upon the magic scene! But of course Harry Potter was not welcomed in with open arms to this world because he was a wizard; the word 'wizard' was said in hushed tones, if spoken at all; it was a dirty word and all wizards in this magical space were looked down upon, often from a magic carpet!

'I've only been on the street five minutes and already I'm in a magician's bad books; still, could be worse, worse than worse, in fact,' Benjamin smiled, paraphrasing a certain ogre giant in a magical book about wizards, for he could be in the bad books of a wizard gone bad!

Benjamin thought it very refreshing there weren't any wizards on this magical street apart from a magician named Wizenbaum, for in his world a few years earlier you couldn't walk down the street without bumping into a wizard. That wasn't quite true but it wasn't far from the truth; these imaginary wizards were often seen reading a book, a magical story, obviously, so magical they could not put it down, as if it was stuck to their hands. They clearly imagined they were not there on the street, they had been sucked into a magical world, by the power of the storyteller, a magician, trickster, conjuror, who could hold you spellbound, make the real world disappear at least for a magical moment or three. These were moments, magical moments to those under the spell of the story, which appeared to last a lifetime. Magical stories stayed with you for a lifetime and if that wasn't magic then Benjamin did not know what was; the magic of the mind, the real magic trapped inside the magic trunk inside your head until you uttered the magic word 'Abracadabra!' then, hey presto, the magic would appear before you, exactly like magic.

Benjamin waited patiently for the first magician to work his magic in his tiny but magical space of the advent calendar, a small doorstop theatre, which is how Benjamin was imagining this tiny space. But nothing happened; perhaps it wasn't Christmas time, a magical time when anything seemed possible, so much so, Benjamin had once thought that this may be the only day of the year he was able to perform magic without it going bad. Yes, he would be like the other great magician, Father Christmas, who was only able to work his magic one day a year. A magician who only worked one day a year would soon end up in the Victorian poorhouse; most magicians didn't make a small fortune, only the very best were able to live on a mansion house on Easy Street. One day's work on a magical street like Abracadabra Street and you were made for life, for Benjamin imagined all the best agents and promoters flocked to this magical street talent-spotting.

For Benjamin Blackstone, this was simply wishful thinking on his part; he couldn't do magic on Christmas Day or any other day of the year, and so far he hadn't shown any sign of being blessed with the magic touch, even on a magical street such as this one, Abracadabra Street.

The advent calendar in his mind stayed shut; now, he couldn't even perform magic of the mind. The magic Victorian popup book had performed the magic in the attic, not he, for Benjamin Blackstone was certainly no Harry Houdini, not even a poor man's, poor boy's, Harry Potter. The book entitled *Abracadabra Street* was the magician; he wasn't even the beautiful assistant.

The giant calendar of magicians past disappeared, to be replaced by plain old windows which slammed shut, causing flakes of white paint to fall on the street so, for a second at least, it appeared to be snowing. The whole shop appeared to shiver then shake as if the house itself was alive. Benjamin certainly was shaking in his boots or at least his boots were shaking, causing him to shake as he imagined a giant magician appearing out of the house shaking his fist violently in Benjamin's exact direction.

For a split-second, Benjamin imagined an earthquake, one that would rip up Abracadabra Street as if it were made of paper, as all the magicians now standing on the street would go on a wild ride on a black magic carpet into the stars, never to be seen again. Benjamin really needed to stop his imagination taking him on a wild flight of fancy; he must keep his feet on the ground once again; easier said than done when you find yourself on Abracadabra Street.

Benjamin got the feeling that, in this world, wizard-type magic was frowned upon – a last resort for the poor, average or simply downright bad magician, bad as in 'not very good' rather than Voldemort bad! A wizard in this world was seen as a poor man's magician and one who, like a child in a Victorian storybook, should be seen and not heard; better still, not seen and not heard.

Wouldn't life be easy if all you had to do was wave a magic wand and all your problems would disappear exactly like magic! Benjamin did not find himself wishing he had fallen into a children's storybook where magic was as easy as reciting your ABC; where it was, in fact, child's play. Benjamin did not wish but he desperately wanted to be a real magician and not a wizard who only had to wish or wave their hand like a magic wand to get anything their little hearts desired. Wonders and magic were things not worth having if they came too easily. They had to be earned; it was the way of things. At least these were the thoughts of Benjamin Blackstone, would-be magician; let the cards fall where they may and if those cards turned out to be Tarot Cards and a giant pack collapsed and buried him alive, so be it. It was in the lap of the gods and not the Ancient Greek gods who loved playing silly games; it was in the lap of the gods of magic, *mageia*. If the Tarot Card Magician turned over the Fortune Card then Benjamin's tag of World's Worst Magician would be replaced by World's Best Magician.

Benjamin Blackstone was like a kid in a candy store, or at least a kid in a sweet shop, a magical sweet shop at that, just the sort of sweet shop you would find in a children's storybook. He felt like he did on Christmas Eve as a young child, that wonder and magic were just around the corner, sure that, when he awoke, snow would be everywhere and he would be surrounded by a giant magic circle of white. He was a child in bed in a magic popup book called Christmas Eve and when the clock struck midnight his bed would fly like a magic carpet, landing in another magical popup book entitled Christmas Day. It was often the anticipation of what was to come, whereas sometimes, in the real world, that magic failed to deliver on all it had promised. You could dress Christmas up with tinsel, glitter and Christmas trees but that didn't necessarily make it a magical day. Old-time Victorian Christmases, Benjamin imagined, were far more magical than the modern commercialised Christmases. Boy, was he sounding old, while at the same time sounding like the old penny-pinching Ebenezer Scrooge! The trouble with Benjamin Blackstone, apart from the fact he couldn't do magic to save his life, was that he was an old-time schoolboy, sure that the days of magic had passed him by. That was until a magic book fell into his possession and on the turn of a card, the Fortune Card in a pack of Tarot Cards, everything had changed.

7

Mind Magic

Benjamin was now having trouble making up his mind which magic shop to go into first, as if he was caught in a shower of magic, too much magic for one boy to cope with all on his own. He paced up and down the street with his hands behind his back with a look of a soul who was totally bewildered by all the choices set before him. This was understandable given the fact Benjamin was prone to dress things up that weren't so magical; if he tried to dress these magic shops up, and their proprietors, his head was more likely than not going to explode. This regrettable incident would cause fireworks that were no more magical in this world than the ones in his world. Fireworks that were forever popping up here, there and everywhere, once again taking the magic out of something magical, like fireworks.

Benjamin then crossed the road and wandered up and down the other side of the street, still unable to make up his mind as if he half imagined the magic shops in his mind could not match the ones in reality. 'Reality!' he laughed. Who was he trying to kid?

What with all the excitement, it was understandable that Benjamin didn't know whether he was coming or going. Half of his body wanted to be coming, the other half going; he felt like the lady in the magic routine – Sawing the Lady in Half. In the end, Benjamin walked into the middle of the street, avoiding the magicians flying past his head on magic carpets. Some of the magicians were performing their acts to people who were gathered on the pavement, whooping and hollering as the magicians took their magic act on the road, or to the street, in this extraordinary case. Horses pulling carts piled high with magic tricks and illusions clattered along the cobbled stone street with cries of 'Giddy up Merlin' or 'Giddy up Houdini', the names of the work horses. One of these tricks was the 'Sawing the Lady in Half' illusion. There was one thing missing from this Victorian street – horse manure – but then again, as this was a magical street, no doubt it vanished no sooner than the horse had done its business.

Benjamin spun round in circles like a Victorian top or a whirling dervish or, as he was imagining, the Magic Robot in the children's quiz game. After three spins, three being the magic number, he stopped, his hand pointing outwards as if casting a spell. The magic shop he was pointing to was called Matilda's Magic Store. A woman – a woman magician – he'd never heard of a female magician before. Benjamin could feel himself going red; he wasn't very good when it came to talking to the female of the species; this was probably why he had never had the courage to find a beautiful assistant for his magic act. In truth, Benjamin's magic act was imaginary, which meant all of his beautiful assistants were imaginary; talking to imaginary girls and women he had no trouble with, in fact he was quite the ladies' man, a real dandy like John Joseph Merlin, the maker of automatons and clocks of a most magical nature. This was one man who could be said to be a wizard; he certainly had a wizard's name, Merlin, and surely it was just a matter of time before Merlin the Magician popped up on Abracadabra Street by magic.

Benjamin straightened his attire, flattened down his hair with his hand, gulped down hard and put his best foot forward. Unfortunately, he found it was his worse foot he had put forward and he tripped. Thankfully, he fell onto a magic carpet that was just coming in to land. 'Sorry, boy, all magic carpet flights are grounded for the rest of the day; there's snow on the way!' the man laughed as he pointed to a weather barometer hanging around his neck and the needle which read 'SNOW!'

Benjamin apologised as he strode manfully towards the magic show owned by Matilda Blackstock. As she had half his surname – black – he wondered if she was the sort of woman who suffered from black moods like his father. Perhaps she practised black magic; if she did, she must have a book on Tarot Cards in her shop – a book he must have. That way, he would be able to understand better the cards the Tarot Magician was more likely than not to be holding up to his face as this story got up a good head of steam.

As usual, Benjamin was over-thinking everything; he tried to make his mind go blank; that was the only way he would have the courage to enter the shop. As Benjamin reached for the door, everything once again appeared to stop stock still, including time.

The magic shops were no longer made of red bricks and mortar, they were made of cardboard; the shops were like the giant facades on movie sets with nothing behind them. Facades were something Benjamin knew all about, putting on a show, appearing more confident than you really were when you wanted a black hole to open and swallow you up.

This is how Benjamin felt the few times he had gone on stage, as stage fright took over his whole body. He felt like a ventriloquist's dummy, but there was no ventriloquist on the stage to work this dummy. Thankfully, his father was under the stage working the lift and the trapdoor, so Benjamin was swallowed up before he even got a chance to get his first stuttering words out. This act of a father saving his son from a fall, a pratfall, had actually got a good laugh; the audience presumed it was all a part of his act – a comic magician. Unfortunately, after the third false start, the audience got wise and started a slow hand clap as Benjamin was booed off the stage with his black tailed frock coat between his legs. Three wasn't always the magic number!

Benjamin coughed loudly three times; this was a signal to his brain to work its mind magic act, fooling Benjamin into believing he could do anything if he simply believed. Suddenly, the shop in front of him began to shrink, or perhaps he was growing in confidence. Abracadabra, hey presto, the old mind trick was working. He was now on the Doorstep Theatre, as his grandfather called it, which is how his grandfather practised his magic tricks to anybody who appeared on the family doorstop. Grandfather Blackstone told Benjamin this improved his stage patter no end and his sleight-of-hand tricks, although pickpocketing various items out of the pockets of door-to-door salesmen, gas men, plumbers and conmen was fun. It wasn't quite so fun when his grandfather lifted the pocket watch of a detective who was going door to door asking if anybody had seen an escapee from the local prison. Thankfully, being a budding escapologist like his hero,

Harry Houdini, his grandfather had got out of the handcuffs the police had put on him to teach him a lesson.

Shops in stories about magic were often small on the outside and vast on the inside; perhaps this magic shop was different; perhaps it was the other way around.

8

Madam Matilda

It must have appeared to the other customers that this boy had walked into this shop in his sleep, for Benjamin's eyes were closed in acute concentration as he entered. That was until the doorbell rang loudly behind him, sounding more like the chimes of Big Ben than a simple doorbell. Benjamin almost jumped out of his thin skin as he opened his eyes wide like a startled animal to see the whole shop staring back at him. Whereas before, Benjamin's appearance was flushed, now it was positively glowing, like the red nose on Rudolph the Reindeer, either that or Dorothy's sparkling ruby-red slippers.

'Can I help you, sir?' asked a woman dressed in black as she brushed the other customers to one side. Benjamin felt so hot he felt he may suffer from a rare case of Spontaneous Human Combustion. This rare occurrence normally only happened in

Victorian novels or stories set in Victorian England; if it was a trick, it was some trick, or perhaps a magician's very last trick as he tried to go out with a bang!

The woman looked more like a man dressed in black with short black hair and she was scowling as Benjamin imagined the woman to be a black widow, a giant spider, not a widow who, like Queen Victoria, was permanently dressed in black for she was mourning her husband. Perhaps boys were not allowed in the magic store, although she had addressed him as 'sir'; this he felt sure was not the case. Benjamin looked down at his shoes, something young men with little confidence or self-belief often did. He could do with a shoeshine boy to shine his shoes, dirty from his trek through the country to get to his great-grandfather's old house. They said the past was another country; it seemed the attic was another country also, for both seemed a million miles away at this moment in time. While his eyes were looking down, Benjamin noticed there was a lot of dust on the floor; this must be magic dust as he could not see a fairy in sight. It soon became clear this was another illusion created by the imaginative mind, as Benjamin heard several loud sneezes and looked up to see two gentlemen with silver snuff boxes in their hands having partaken in a pinch of snuff to clear the nose.

Benjamin made eye contact with this strange and alluring woman, as if, in no time at all, she had him under her spell. Suddenly, the woman smiled at Benjamin, which changed her whole appearance, at least in Benjamin's eyes, for he could see how pretty she was. Finally, he could let out the breath, one he had been holding onto ever since he stepped into this magical space, half in awe and wonder, half in fright. It felt to Benjamin as if he had been wearing a straightjacket; perhaps he needed to get himself one, a fashionably attired straightjacket, if he was going to look presentable when the authorities carted him off to the nearest madhouse.

Where was the nearest madhouse? That was a good question and one that deserved a good answer: Hatter Street, just round the corner, and upon the street was a hat shop named Mad Hatters. A madman wanted to look their best when entering a madhouse. Benjamin might already be in a madhouse, and he didn't mean the magic shop, he meant his great-grandfather Atticus Blackstone's mansion, with its magical attic, the one which was now keeping him prisoner against his will.

'My, those who practise magic are getting younger and younger, it makes me feel positively ancient,' the woman laughed, then introduced herself. 'My name's Matilda, sorry, as most of my customers are older men I think they are a little put out by such a good-looking young man.'

'Good-looking? I don't know about that,' Benjamin found himself saying in a manner which made him sound very grown up. He glanced over to a looking glass in the shop; the reflection in the mirror winked at him. Benjamin touched his face; he must have a nervous tic because he most certainly hadn't winked, it must be a magic mirror – that was it – a magic mirror. Benjamin smiled; he was good-looking, funny, and beautiful women wanted to talk to him – this street really must be a magical one unless this was all a surreal dream.

'You're new around here, aren't you? I've never seen you before,' Matilda said looking a little puzzled. 'Oh dear, that sounds as if I'm playing to an audience and you're a member of that audience who has just stepped up onto the stage.'

'In which case I suppose I should reply, I have never seen you before in my life, madam,' Benjamin replied with this rather witty line as he felt himself growing taller by the second like a flower in a time-lapse nature documentary. The attic no longer had him under its spell; now he was under the spell of a witch, bewitched, in fact, in the presence of the woman named Matilda. This lightning-fast growing spurt was not down to magic, as Benjamin's hair hadn't start to magically grow; it was simply a boy growing in confidence. Benjamin may well be under a spell, a love spell.

However, Benjamin did not think this was the case. 'Let me introduce myself; my name's Benjamin H. Blackstone, a part of the Blackstone family magicians and magic-makers for 300 years. I'm not 300 years old,' Benjamin added hastily for he had many a book on magic where wizened wizards still practised magic at the grand old age of 500, some even older.

'If you were you certainly have aged well, I take it you've been taking a magic potion, the Elixir of Life.' Matilda giggled so much that Benjamin wondered if the woman was younger than she looked or older. Benjamin checked his appearance in the looking glass again, hoping he wasn't getting older by the second. Thankfully, this was not the extraordinary case, for if he got any younger he may well give Benjamin Button a run for his money.

Baby magicians, child prodigies in prams doing magic tricks, was a rare sight indeed – perhaps not on Abracadabra Street? Benjamin's baby brother Alex was already a practising magician having performed a nice 'now you see it, now you don't' trick using a dummy. This made his mother age overnight, for she was sure her baby son had swallowed the dummy; his father had smiled when he heard this and cried theatrically, 'That's my boy, he's going to be the best magician in the illustrious history of the Blackstone family, one who will restore the family name of Blackstone to its former glory, Magic Circle here we come!'

This made Benjamin feel even smaller as he shrank to the size of the freak show midget Major Tom Thumb. His baby brother Alexander was already pulling off magic tricks in his pram with effortless ease as if he was the young Harry Potter and he, Benjamin H. Blackstone, could barely pull off the trick of walking and talking without tripping over his tongue or his big left feet! But that was no longer the case as Benjamin began to feel the magic flowing through his whole body like an electric current. He was sure his hair was standing on end like fairy sparks, static electricity, but this time he didn't check his appearance in the looking glass in the shop for he did not want to appear vain. He'd check it later. When he produced an old Victorian hand admirer from his pocket, exactly like magic, everyone in the shop stopped what they were doing and applauded wildly.

'I could do with a young man who practises magic. I have an idea for a magic act: two young magicians, one male, the other female. I want to do away with the old-school approach of the man being the magician and the woman being the beautiful assistant, simply a distraction so the magician can pull off whatever trick or illusion he is trying to pull off. It's always been the same; a man cannot work without a strong woman standing behind him, often in the shadows. Well, I want to see a strong woman next to that male magician. Perhaps one day even standing in front of the magician as the magician is a woman and the man is her beautiful assistant.'

For a moment, a most magical moment, Benjamin thought Matilda had him in mind for the beautiful, or at least handsome, assistant to the female magician. In truth he wouldn't have minded this a bit; he did not see it as some other magicians would have done, as a slur against his good name, for he didn't have a good name. The name of Blackstone, thanks to his great-grandfather Atticus Blackstone, had blackened the family name so much that Benjamin who had expected his giant black shadow to overshadow him even in this world.

In truth, if he became the beautiful assistant, he wouldn't have to practise magic which he was bad at; he could simply distract the audience with his stunning good looks and charm. It was money for old rope and you could forget the Indian rope trick, for Benjamin didn't much care for heights or the slippery snake-oil salesman/magician who had first greeted him when he landed on Abracadabra Street. Benjamin certainly appeared to have landed on his feet all right, feet that no longer felt like they belonged to a baby elephant or the storyteller Hans Christian Andersen who had size thirteen feet, unlucky in his case, for he was said to resemble a giant stork.

'Would you like to come and work for me, Benjamin? I will teach you all I know and, despite being a woman, a female magician, and the only one I know, I can teach you a lot,' said Matilda, her emerald-green eyes sparkling so brightly he felt well and truly under her spell.

'I... I would be honoured,' Benjamin replied, wondering if he should kiss the gloved hand of the woman wearing a velvet opera glove done up with a gold button. No, that would look silly; after all, he was only a boy, wasn't he? The desire to look into the mirror was almost too strong; it was as if the looking glass was compelling him to look into it. 'Harry Potter, eat your heart out,' Benjamin coughed under his breath. Frankly, he could have said it over his breath, given the fact wizards in this world were looked down upon.

'Harry who?' Matilda enquired, looking a little puzzled.

'Harry Houdini, he's one of my heroes,' Benjamin replied, hoping he had covered his tracks for he was 1000% sure Matilda had never heard of Harry Potter, for it was clear he was now in the times of the Victorians or the Edwardians. The magic popup book named Abracadabra Street his great-grandfather found in an antiquarian bookshop in Hungary was, after all, Victorian memorabilia, Victoriana in fact. Given this fact, Benjamin was sure the woman who owned the magic shop, Madam Matilda, had heard of Erich Weiss, aka Harry Houdini.

'Harry Houdini, sorry, never heard of him, is he any good?' Matilda asked, her face as straight as a magic wand.

'Is he any good!' exclaimed Benjamin, keeping this exclamation to himself: *he was only the greatest illusionist of all time!* 'He's very, very good,' Benjamin stuttered, only meaning to say 'very good', although Harry Houdini was very, very, very good. Rub that last line out; he was great, the Great Harry Houdini the Master Magician; it said so on the old movie poster Benjamin had on his bedroom wall.

Benjamin wanted to tell Matilda that his middle name was Harry, named after the great Harry Houdini, who obviously in this neck of the woods wasn't so great, as the woman did not appear to have heard of him. This was Abracadabra Street wasn't it? How could Matilda not have heard of one of the greatest illusionist escapologists of all time?

'Sorry Benjamin, only teasing, of course I've heard of Harry Houdini, he was only in my shop last week after which he went on a flying visit to Europe; not on a magic carpet, I hasten to add, on the famed Orient Express.' Matilda smiled, taking Benjamin by the arm. 'Now, I'm going to introduce you to a very special young lady named Scarlet; you will be working closely with her as part of the double act, a magic double act. I suppose I'll have to think of a name for the pair of you; I dare say the name will come to me as if by magic just when I least expect it.'

The grimace vanished and the smile returned as once again Benjamin Blackstone was walking on air; in fact he imagined he and Matilda were both walking on air passing over the customers in the shop. Then they disappeared up through a trapdoor in the ceiling and into the attic on the top floor as if by magic. Benjamin's world really had been turned upside down for the trapdoor was normally in the floor, not in the ceiling.

This magical disappearing act was simply wishful thinking on young Master Blackstone's part – the magic of the mind – as there wasn't an attic in this magic shop, or if there was, it was invisible at least from the outside. Perhaps there was a false bottom in the shop or at least a cellar?

All magic shops were magical through the eyes of a magician or conjurer, but some magic shops were more magical than others. Benjamin already believed this was one of the more magical magic shops and that was saying something given the fact it was standing on a magical street named Abracadabra Street. What Benjamin hadn't yet realised was that, across the other side of the street, mirroring Matilda's Magic Shop, was Harry Houdini's Magic Shop, and next door to his, Robert Houdin's Magic Shop. Houdini and Houdin's magic shops were linked by a mirrored wardrobe which led from one shop to the other. This may well have surprised Benjamin, for in his world, Harry Houdini and Robert Houdin had never met. In fact, Harry Houdini had asked Houdin's widow if he could visit his hero's grave, but she refused. After this, Houdini made it his business to tear down Robert Houdin's giant house of cards, one card by one, until the only one left was the card with the depiction of the Grim Reaper. This, to Benjamin's mind, seemed a grave injustice and one that he was sure would have had Robert Houdin turning in his grave. But that was the magic business all over; there was so much secrecy, so much jealousy as a magician, you were always looking over your shoulder.

Robert Houdin and Harry Houdini, aka Erich Weiss, both cast a giant spell and a giant shadow over the world of magic, a shadow that still existed today, although apparently not on Abracadabra Street. Benjamin looked out of the window of Matilda's Magic Shop and saw the two men arm in arm walking out of their shops as if they were the very best of friends. What was that old expression? 'Keep your friends close and your enemies even closer.' Benjamin did not wish to make an enemy of Madam Matilda for it was clear to him she had a mind like a steel trap, and no doubt she had a steel trap set up somewhere in her shop for any man who tried to pull a dirty trick on her. The steel trapdoor, Benjamin imagined, led to a steel box belonging to a magician named Pandora who had long since passed onto the spirit world.

9

No Escape

'Harry! Robert!' Benjamin cried, trying to get the attention of his two heroes, but they did not wave back and why would they? He wasn't a big name in circles that magicians circulated in and given the fact he was the World's Worst Magician, no wonder they wouldn't give him the time of day. Benjamin felt his pocket – that was strange – where had his silver fob watch on its chain gone? He'd only glanced at it a minute ago. Somebody – a pickpocket – must have taken it out of his waistcoat pocket while he was distracted by the two greatest magicians who had ever lived. Then he saw Robert Houdin holding up a fob watch dangling it in front of him from a silver chain as if he was trying to hypnotise somebody. Benjamin, by the look on his face, his eyes as wide as saucers, spinning saucers at that. 'Th… that's my watch!' Benjamin cried, but he was no longer frowning for he'd turned the frown upside down. 'How on earth?'

'Sorry, boy, couldn't help myself,' Robert Houdin cried, flying into the shop on a magic carpet through the open door with Harry Houdini by his side, both men grinning like the Cheshire cat.

'Harry Robert, give the poor boy his watch back, you should be ashamed of yourselves, you must remember when you were magicians wet behind the ears, that's a dirty trick!' Madam Matilda exclaimed, appearing out of thin air or the trapdoor in the floor. 'And when did you get back from your tour of Europe, Harry?'

'I was back before I knew it, even I don't know how magical I am sometimes,' Houdini cried.

'Well apologise to the boy, please,' said Matilda, giving the two men a black look.

'Sorry, Matilda, sorry...' grunted Robert Houdin and Harry Houdini apologetically as Benjamin just about managed to get his jaw off the floor in time.

'B... Benjamin B... Blackstone,' stuttered Benjamin, shrinking visibly before the two men's eyes.

'You're not from the Blackstone family, Atticus Blackstone's great-grandson, are you?' Robert Houdin gasped, almost falling off the magic carpet hovering just off the floor.

Benjamin wanted to say, 'No absolutely not,' but he couldn't tell a lie if his life depended upon it. Like the rest of his family, he was as straight as a magic wand; he felt he had to be, to make up for his great-grandfather's catalogue of dirty underhanded tricks. 'The Great Magic Rip Off!' Benjamin saw a headline in *Magic News* in neon writing flashing on and off before his eyes. 'Yes, yes I am.'

'Poor boy, I feel sorry for you and your family. Atticus Blackstone was a bad egg, a rotten one in truth, stank the Magic

Circle out worse than the Great Victorian Stink, in fact.' Harry Houdini grimaced, shaking his head theatrically. This was the dark magic of synchronicity at work. Benjamin had got to meet his heroes who didn't appear to have feet of clay, more like wings of a dove; he was the one with the feet of clay.

'Last time I saw Atticus the old rogue was in Timbuktu; he could easily disappear there, being dark of skin,' Robert Houdin sniffed.

'Good job Matilda has taken you under her giant wing then; don't let her down, will you, boy? Or you'll have me and Robert to deal with.' Harry Houdini scowled as a black look appeared on his face. Benjamin was now standing in the shop with a black cloud hanging over his head and yes, it was raining, but only on him, on his magic parade – dark magic.

Hold on a moment – not a magic one – what did Robert Houdin say about his great-grandfather? He said he was dark of skin – how was that possible? In all the pictures of his great-grandfather he'd seen, mostly in the mansion belonging to Atticus Blackstone, he was white. In fact, Benjamin had always thought he'd make a good ghost, or a bad one, the more likely Victorian ghost story! Forget holding the moment, that wasn't in the slightest bit magical. Hold the front page of *Magic Monthly* – Atticus Blackstone had pulled off the greatest trick of them all – the Lazarus Trick – coming back from the dead. That wasn't the half of it – his great-grandfather was still alive somewhere in this small world, and possibly still performing his black magic on Abracadabra Street. Had Atticus Blackstone performed the 'Sawing the Lady in Half' routine on himself, thus splitting himself in two? Benjamin needed to get his head read if he believed that last fantastical tale, the one he'd just spun himself. He'd better look up Sigmund Freud, the famous psychoanalyst. The sooner the better by the looks of it, for it was clear he was fast losing his mind.

While all the old/new magic news was sinking in, Harry Houdini and Robert Houdin reversed out of the door on their magic carpet blowing kisses to Madam Matilda, leaving Benjamin feeling as if somebody had pulled both the rug and the magic carpet out from underneath his feet. Did anyone actually walk anywhere? Apparently not on Abracadabra Street. Perhaps it was because the street was the longest street in the world, or perhaps it was because it was such fun to ride upon a magic carpet; only a magical carousel ride could come close.

In the blinking of the Third Eye, Benjamin had managed to get into the bad books of the two greatest magic men of all time; no wonder he'd got the title of World's Worst Magician; he'd earned the title, he'd stunk the magic world out. He was only surprised the men in the shop hadn't hissed and booed and thrown rotten fruit at him as they did in the days of William Shakespeare at the Globe Theatre in London.

Benjamin felt he was both drowning in Harry Houdini's Water Torture Illusion and trying to lift his head off the block it was clearly on, as if he was attempting to lift Robert Houdin's suitcase off the floor. Robert Houdin's trick was a simple one – at first, the suitcase felt as light as a feather, then you placed it upon the ground and asked somebody to pick it up, which they could not, because now it weighed a ton. Houdini had also made an elephant disappear from a crate; Benjamin now found himself wishing Houdini could make the elephant in the room disappear as easily. The elephant in the room, or magic shop in this extraordinary case of imaginary magic, was the fact that Benjamin's great-grandfather was bone black and bad to the bone.

'Don't worry, Benjamin; one day those two great men of magic will be carrying you high upon their shoulders all the way to the Magic Circle and the Magic Hall of Fame, you mark my words. The Blackstone name will be restored and your family will become members of the famed Magic Circle once more,' cried Matilda as she brushed the dark cloud away with her hand as if it were a magic wand.

Benjamin had wondered if Matilda and the two men were in on the trick. Had Matilda removed his watch, Robert Houdin could have then held up a watch and then when the two men had entered the shop, Matilda could have passed Benjamin's fob watch to Robert Houdin. If this was the case, it was a dirty trick, but no he couldn't – wouldn't – think Madam Matilda could be so unkind. Benjamin chastised himself for even doubting his mentor; perhaps it was his great-grandfather's evil spirit getting into him? He certainly hoped not; one black sheep in the family was enough.

Benjamin begged to be excused and stepped back onto the street, for he was eager to see what other magic shops had popped up while his back was turned. Hopefully he wouldn't be robbed blind by some carpet baggers trying to sell him a magic carpet which was nothing more than a moth-eaten rug!

10

Merlin Magician or Tin Pot Wizard?

'I don't believe it – Merlin's Cave and Merlin's Mechanical Marvels!' said Benjamin as these two shops popped up, side by side, on the street, exactly like magic.

Benjamin almost fell flat on his face in his hurry to meet the greatest magician of all time, Merlin the Magician. As misfortune would have it, the owner of Merlin's Cave, Merlin the Magician, was out to lunch. Benjamin surmised the great magician was probably dinning out with King Arthur and his Knights of the Round Table in Avalon, a most magical space. *Still, no matter*, thought Benjamin, *I shall enter Merlin's Mechanical Marvels, which belonged to a wizard named John Joseph Merlin*. It was in fact a museum of all his famous mechanical automatons and clocks. Time seemed to slow down in this shop, as did the clocks. Once again, Benjamin was out of luck as J.J. Merlin was also out to lunch, leaving his able assistant, himself in the form of a mechanical man, an automaton, to serve the customers.

'Can... can I help... help you, sir,' the mechanical man asked as Benjamin stepped up to the counter. Did J.J. Merlin have a stutter or was the tin pot magic man in need of a little oiling? 'Oil the wheels' was an old expression which in essence meant making small talk, listening to others and praising them to the hilt even when they weren't worthy of praise, or so Benjamin's father once told him, when oiling the wheels of one of his own mechanical marvels. Clearly, this mechanical man was no Magic Robot, a game Benjamin often played with his family on dark rainy days. Some of the children teased Benjamin at school, calling him the Magic Robot, for he was so wooden of gait at times, almost as if he was a clockwork toy. This was hardly an insult given the fact the Magic Robot had been the Brain of Britain since the game first came on the market back in the 1950s.

If Benjamin was looking for work so he could stand on his own two feet on Abracadabra Street, he could offer to play the part of the Magic Robot – dress up in a mechanical-looking suit if needs be and talking in a robotic fashion – the customers in the shop would love it.

'Magic derives from the Greek word *mageia*; the Persians invented magic in the first century AD, so wrote the Pliny the Elder. Magic was first discovered by ancient philosopher Zoroaster in 647 BC but was only written down in the fifth century BCE by magician Osthanes. The Iota Bowl is the oldest magic trick in the world, dating from around 3000 BCE. The trick involves a vessel that is able to empty itself and then refill itself. The trick to magic is the hand deceiving the eye and the mind. I made that last one up, but I won't charge you extra for the humour,' the Magic Robot named Benjamin

Blackstone continued to spit out facts on magic without any help from magic mushrooms!

When magic carpet rides were freely available in this magical world, there really seemed no point standing on your own two feet!

'Yes, yes, I… I think you… you can,' stuttered Benjamin. He wasn't trying to make fun of the tin man built in Merlin's image or at least J.J. Merlin's image, it was just if someone started stuttering, it set the wheels in motion for him to do likewise.

The mechanical man did not reply, for he appeared to have run out of steam.

'S… sorry I've changed my mind, I don't want to speak to the monkey, I want to speak to the organ grinder,' said Benjamin, hardly believing the words coming out of his own mouth. 'S… sorry I don't know what I'm saying,' stuttered Benjamin, appearing not to know his own mind, the self-impelling steam wheel of the mind, turning first clockwise then anti-clockwise.

Benjamin spun on his heels giving the Victorian villain Spring-Heeled Jack a run for his money as he ran for the door. As he did, he saw a sign on the shop door: 'Closed for Repairs'. The shop then began to fold up in what can only be described as a mechanical fashion, a mechanical Pandora's Box was how Benjamin would have described this nightmare if he hadn't been tongue-tied. Alternatively (and after all this was an alternate reality), perhaps a mechanical house of cards that folded up – another wild imagining from the magic trunk in Benjamin Blackstone's mind. Benjamin stared wild-eyed as he disappeared into a world of darkness, wondering if he'd ever see the light of day again.

11

The Wheel of Misfortune

Benjamin cautiously opened one eye then the other, trying not to fear the worst in case he brought the worst on himself. How could he bring the worst on himself? For was not Benjamin Blackstone already the self-titled World's Worst Magician? Benjamin heard a cacophony of voices; the room was poorly lit, almost as if he were in a cave. Benjamin may have stunk the joint and the theatre out as a magician, but as a detective, he wasn't half bad, for his instincts were right: he was in a cave, Merlin's Cave.

'Looks like we have a customer,' said an old wizened man with a long grey beard. Of course, Benjamin's first thought was this must be a secret meeting of wizards who, after all, were banished to the shadows in this world full of great magicians. Perhaps that was why this small circle of wizards appeared to be welcoming him in with open arms?

'Fancy a brew?' asked the man, stirring what Benjamin naturally thought was a wizard's brew until the man passed him a cup of tea. Okay, so he wasn't that hot as a detective either. Unless the tea was a small wizard's brew – black dragon tea – one sip and he would turn into a wizard! The thought appalled Benjamin. A wizard, of all things. He'd rather be turned into a warty toad than a wizard with a wart on the end of his long pointy hooked nose! In the Orient, tea was thought to be a magical substance – dragon tea in particular. Sprinkled on an object, it would transform that object into something magical.

'Thank you, I'm good,' Benjamin replied, feeling anything but good; still, at least he was oiling the wheels, making small talk, however small that talk was.

'I heard on the magical grapevine – the street – for I always have my ear to the street,' the man said, 'that you wished to meet me, so here I am, warts and all,' the man said, then added, 'my name's Merlin the Magician.'

'Of course you are,' Benjamin laughed, unable to help himself for he did not believe for one moment this was Merlin the Magician. There were many men in his world, pagan warlocks, calling themselves Merlin, there was even one a stone's throw away, next door in fact, a tin pot wizard named Merlin. Not much of a magician or a wizard, for he couldn't even manage to work himself!

'So why did you wish to meet me?' Merlin asked, scratching his back with what looked like a long magic wand.

It was true, Benjamin had wished to meet one of his heroes, but surely this wish had been purely wishful thinking on his part. The last thing he wanted to do was bring this magical world down upon his head for disrespecting the greatest magic man of them all. This was Abracadabra Street; why couldn't one of his wishes come true? If this was indeed a fact and not a far-fetched fiction then it meant... drum roll... he could do magic! Benjamin Harry Blackstone could, like Harry Houdini and Robert Houdin, perform magic, magic of the mind. Hold on, Houdini and Houdin couldn't perform real magic. Benjamin Blackstone, like the wizard boy who lived, Harry Potter. What was he saying? Harry Potter was only a character in a storybook. He wasn't real, made of flesh and blood, like Benjamin Blackstone who was... a character in a book entitled *Abracadabra Street*. Both books were clearly magical storybooks, for both Harry and Benjamin appeared to be so lifelike they had literally popped out of the books themselves, exactly like magic. Let it be known, from this day forth, that Master Benjamin H. Blackstone of the Blackstone family of magicians and magic makers could perform real magic.

But didn't that make Benjamin a... don't say that word, it's not a magic word... I said don't say that word... WIZARD! Benjamin couldn't help himself exclaiming, 'I am a W-I-Z-A-R-D!'

'SSSSSSSHHHHHH!' the room appeared to cry or at least the circle of wizards in the room, cave, shop, whatever it was, possible a library – the Lost Library of Timbuktu, the most magical library of all time. That could be debated for the Lost Library of Alexandria was said to be a most magical library, as was another lost library in South America where a library of golden books was hidden. Up to this point in time, the library had not popped up as if by magic; perhaps one day it would pop up, exactly like magic?

Benjamin noticed a large wheel on the wall; it looked like one of those Wheels of Fortune you saw in game shows except on closer inspection Benjamin noticed it had spikes sticking out of it. 'Never judge a book by its cover and never judge a Wheel of Fortune by its appearance,' Benjamin muttered to himself, feeling the walls and the room close in on him, so that it felt as if he was now inside a magic trunk, no doubt one that once upon a time belonged to a wizardess named Pandora.

'Get the boy, he's a wizard-hater!' cried a man dressed in black robes and a black pointy hat, one Benjamin imagined was covered in black stars as a hundred shadows appeared out of the walls. Before he knew it, Benjamin was tied to the Wheel of Fortune – Wheel of Misfortune was the more likely story!

12

Black Magic

Now Benjamin was standing in front of what looked like a firing squad of Shadow Wizards, but instead of firearms, in their hands they had magic wands.

'W... what are you going to do with me?' stuttered Benjamin, trembling with fear, trying not to fear the worst in case he brought the worst on himself. It was probably too late for that; he'd already brought the worst on himself as soon as he stepped into the attic in his great-grandfather's haunted house!

'We are going to teach you a lesson you won't forget, although as you won't live very long after we have finished with you I wouldn't worry too much about it!' cackled one of the Shadow Wizards as he threw his wand at Benjamin as if it were a dart or an arrow. Instinctively, Benjamin shut his eyes and turned his head away. The wand flew like the quiver of a bowman's arrow, striking the Wheel of Misfortune, missing Benjamin's ear by a hair's breadth. The wand was thrown with such force, the arrow was still quivering in the wood a minute after it had struck its intended target.

Benjamin did not think this was true, for he was sure the Shadow Wizards were trying to hit him, although as this was clearly a medieval torture device, no doubt they were trying to scare him first, or perhaps they were trying to scare him to death. Being Scared to Death was right up there with Spontaneous Human Combustion for an unusual death for all writers of horror and ghost stories, of which the Victorians were so fond.

Then another wand flew through the air, and another and another; the third arrow stuck and pieced his right ear. Benjamin winced but did not cry out. If he was going to die he was going to die like a magician. The only good wizard in Benjamin Blackstone's book was a dead wizard!

'If you pierce the boy's other ear he can become a pirate and sail the Seven Black Seas with Captain Blood and Captain Bluebeard!' laughed one of the Shadow Wizards, sharpening his wand on a stone. As it appeared to Benjamin, the end of the wands had metal tips; perhaps these tips were even dipped in poison? Benjamin began to feel light-headed, woozy, he was not sure if this was because he hated the sight of blood, especially he own (old joke, black humour – well, if you're going to die on stage you may as well die laughing!) or because the tips of the wands really had been dipped in poison.

'Should have pierced his black heart. I blame this glass eye!' spat the Shadow Wizard, about to cast another wand out of his wand quiver.

'The Order of the Wizards of Shadows will make you pay!' growled another wizard, which Benjamin thought was a little bit theatrical as his mind tried to soften the blow by using humour black humour as a weapon.

'I... I brought this on myself, didn't I?' said Benjamin, half talking to himself and half asking the Shadow Wizards the question, the one he was sure he already knew the answer to.

'Of course you did, boy, mischievous elves certainly are not responsible this time round. Wizards not only have eyes in the back of their heads,' grunted the Shadow Wizard turning round to prove he wasn't making this up as two coal-black cold eyes stared back at Benjamin giving him the old evil eye, 'we also have the gift of the Third Eye, the all-seeing eye. We can see in worlds you cannot even imagine, dark worlds, darker than this one, far darker.'

Benjamin did his best not to think of a certain professor with eyes in the back of his head – Professor Quiver, as Benjamin had named him, for he appeared scared of his own shadow. Benjamin had never been scared of his own shadow but he was scared of the Shadow Wizards who he imagined could cast a thousand shadows of all shapes and sizes. Benjamin imagined a wild cat would jump out of one of the cloaks of a Shadow Wizard and tear him to shreds, the Arabian death of a thousand cuts, and not paper cuts either, as old school storytellers often suffered! Benjamin didn't mind suffering for his art, the Art of Magic, but this was going too far; if this was a test he feared he would fail it. Still, at least he would hold onto his title of the World's Worst Magician!

'The pen is mightier than the sword!' Benjamin cried out, sure the next wand had his name on it: Benjamin H. Blackstone 2015–2027 – DRIP. DRIP for 'Don't Rest In Peace'! Benjamin conjured the sword suit from the deck of Tarot Cards in his mind, hoping it would pop out of thin air and cut him free or cut him to ribbons – red ribbons. There are fifty-six major cards in the Tarot Card deck divided into four suits: wands, swords, pentangles and cups.

Benjamin wished he could throw away the wands, the ones that would be heading his way any minute now! More wishful thinking from the Joker of Wishful Thinking! Then a string of Tarot Cards flew out of his head: the Hanging Man – throw it away; the Justice Card – rough justice and injustice; the Devil – they were all standing in front of him now, their eyes burning with fire; the Tower, the Temperance, the Chariot – he wished it would whisk him away to anywhere, as long as it wasn't the Coliseum in Rome where the lions were making a meal of the Christians. The Hermit card raised its ugly head – he was the hermit; he had spent half his life in his bedroom trying to perfect his magic act and failing miserably. Finally, the last card appeared out of his dark mind. It was the Fool, and there you have it, for it was clear as a crystal ball: Benjamin Blackstone was fooling himself, a clever sleight-of-hand conjuring trick of the mind, a delusion.

Without a shadow of a doubt, Benjamin Blackstone was a magician in name only, living off the family name of Blackstone. *Shadow Wizards, do your worst, put an end to the miserable life of Benjamin Blackstone, not worthy of the name Blackstone or worthy of the ancient art of magic.* The inner voice of Benjamin Blackstone groaned, the weight of the magic world upon his frail shoulders.

'The pen may well be mightier than the sword; unfortunately, the wand – especially in the hand of a wizard – is mightier than either the pen or the sword!' exclaimed the Shadow. Then, just as he was about to let his wand fly – for these wands no doubt had a mind of their own, or so Benjamin imagined – a giant cast a shadow over the whole cave, one dwarfing the Shadow Wizards. *Was this giant shadow that of a giant or an ogre?* thought Benjamin, wondering if he was about to go from the frying pan into the fire, metaphorically speaking.

'You can stick that wand where the sun doesn't shine!' cried Benjamin, defiant to the end, an end only a dark wizard with words could conjure from their dark mind.

'Okay boys, you've had your fun, now let the poor man's magician and poor man's wizard go; he might be a wizard-hater but he is a wizard with words, and that, in my book of magic, counts for something,' cried out a voice from the shadow as the wizards laid down their wands and untied Benjamin, much to his relief.

'You said you brought this on yourself, Master Blackstone, and I suppose in a way you did, but not through any magic or magic of the mind, so I hate to break the spell you're under, although I would imagine you are glad I did. It was I, a master spell-maker, Merlin the Magician, the Greatest Magician who ever lived. I conjured up the spell that brought you into my inner circle. You see, Master Blackstone, I actually wished to meet you and, after all, you are the World's Worst Magician; you said so yourself. Surely you're not so delusional as to believe this dark magic was down to you? We wizards are a mischievous lot at the worst of times and this, for wizards, I'm afraid is the worst of times, an age of Magicians, while we wizards are left in the dark, and what can be a darker place than a cave?' Merlin smiled, baring a set of white pearly teeth that almost blinded Benjamin, then sighed as it appeared he too was wearing a crooked smile, one side of his face smiling, the other grimacing.

Something was clearly blinding Benjamin Blackstone and he didn't think it was the truth! But he did want to find the truth and somewhere in his befuddled mind he imagined that Merlin the Magician would be able to tell him what he wanted to know. And what Benjamin wanted to know was how it was his great-grandfather (not so great, which is why Benjamin no doubt was the worst magician in the world) was both black and white.

'Hocus-pocus!' Benjamin grunted, unable to accept a single word that had come out of Merlin the Magician's mouth; it probably wasn't coming out of the mouth of Merlin, it was more likely than not Merlin was another tin pot wizard, an automaton built by John Joseph Merlin. Yes, that was it: Merlin the Magician, not being able to be in thousands of places at the same time on his whistle-stop tour of time and space to please his ever-growing list of fans, asked J.J. Merlin to build him an army of tin pot replica wizards named Merlin!

Benjamin could just about accept the unacceptable fact that his great-grandfather was still alive on this street after being sucked into the Victorian popup book entitled *Abracadabra Street*, for the exact same thing had happened to him. It may have happened to many other magicians, all of whom had been turned to not stone, but cardboard cut-out figures, never being able to leave this world, by the looks of it. But Benjamin could not and would not accept his great-grandfather had the power of a changeling, practised black magic, wore a death mask and stuck pins in straw effigies.

'Your great-grandfather, Atticus Blackstone, had a half-brother almost as black as the Ace of Spades; the two had never met until one day they came face to face on Abracadabra Street, the Victorian London part of the street, just a small street as you can see. At first they were wary of one another but then became the best of friends; they even formed a magic act, using two mirrored wardrobes, not particularly original apart from the mirrors, and instead of Atticus stepping out of the door of the wardrobe across the other side of the stage from which he had stepped into the wardrobe, or should I say his brother Nathan, he then stepped out of the mirror, a trick mirror, naturally.

The act was called 'The Miracle Mirror Man'; of course the act was two men and Atticus had to blacken his face with coal to make the act work, not something he enjoyed doing and not something I agree with, but it is a common enough practice on the Vaudeville circuit.'

'The Ace of Spade in the Tarot Card is also known as the spadille Death Card,' Benjamin spat out the words from his mouth as if he were the Magic Robot, 'and furthermore it is the luckiest card in the pack.' Benjamin wondered if the fact his great-uncle Nathan Blackstone was as black as the Ace of Spades was a lucky omen in his family history or if he, like his great-grandfather Atticus, was another black sheep of the family. In truth, when the history of the Blackstone family was written, Benjamin Blackstone, the World's Worst Magician, would be one of those black sheep, or so he imagined.

'Then what happened?' Benjamin asked, under the spell of the storyteller, hanging on every word that came out of the mouth of Merlin the Magician, who undoubtedly had a silver tongue. Benjamin, being a storyteller himself, could tell the story had an unhappy ending but at least it had an ending, after which he would at least know the truth about his great-grandfather's life. At least up until this point, because clearly he was still alive; perhaps it wasn't the Tarot Card Conjurer shadowing him but his great-grandfather?

'Like a lot of double acts who spent a lot of time around one another, they had a falling out, a big one, and it was over your mentor, Madam Matilda. You see, they were both under her spell, hung on her every word, all she had to do was say the magic word, any word, and her wish was their command. The two brothers fought and by this time Madam Matilda was head over heels in love with another magician. The two brothers parted; one went up Abracadabra Street the other down it, and to my knowledge they have never seen one another since that black day.'

'You obviously know about Atticus selling the family Blackstone secrets, which got the family thrown out of the Magic Circle?' Benjamin pressed the great magician further as the story unfolded like a badly made origami paper boat.

'Atticus… no you've got that all wrong, Atticus never sold any of the Blackstone family secrets and nor did his brother Nathan; but that is a secret I cannot share with you, for in all honesty I am not completely sure,' said Merlin, not sure if he had already said too much and spoken out of turn.

'But you have your suspicions?' said Benjamin, hoping for the final piece of the story puzzle that may set him free and his family from the black stain on their good name.

'Yes I do, but unfortunately I cannot prove it; perhaps that is why you are here,' said Merlin, then said no more.

'S… sorry, I must go; it was nice to meet you, Mr Merlin. I wish you all the best in the future; give my kindest regards to King Arthur,' Benjamin stuttered, then he disappeared out of the cave door, his head spinning like a miniature carousel. Benjamin decided that perhaps those old expressions, 'Be careful what you wish for' and 'Never meet your heroes' held some water, like Houdin's Water Torture Trick. As Benjamin left the cave he heard water dripping off the walls as if the whole cave was a giant water clock. Drip drop, tick tock, drip drop, tick tock, time was running out, as were the sands of time.

Something was telling Benjamin he had to find 'the magic', his personal Holy Grail, before this world collapsed around his ears and he may need to find his great-grandfather and his half-brother if he was to do so, for surely they were the key to this mystery.

13

Blackstone Magic

In the blinking of an eye, Benjamin found himself back on the street looking at his reflection in the window of Merlin's Cave, the magic emporium. The window of Merlin's Cave was jet black, as if the glass was an opening to a cave; this cave did not have a glass ceiling but a sliding door made of glass. The window looked like a large black mirror through the wide eyes of Benjamin Blackstone; in the mirror Benjamin saw a thousand and one stars, not one star more, not one star less.

Did this mean that Benjamin had fallen into another giant magical book, one entitled *A Thousand and One Nights*, the original title of the Arabian Nights? This truly was a magical book in every sense of every word. The book was well over a thousand and one pages long and had been written many, many moons before the Victorian popup book entitled *Abracadabra*

Street was written. In fact, *A Thousand and One Nights* was written exactly a thousand and one years before the Victorian popup book *Abracadabra Street*. An even more unlikely story was there were exactly a thousand pages between the two magical books; actually, that was a fiction, but it sounded like a fact.

'Never judge a book by its cover!' sniffed Benjamin, kicking himself for he was well and truly sucked in under the spell of the Victorian popup book entitled *Abracadabra Street*. The word 'Abracadabra' was a magical word but only in the sense of old-time magic; the word had lost its magic in his world; it was thought to be outdated, even corny, one only party magicians would use in their act.

Abracadabra Street was a book that only had one solitary page in it, but what a magical page and what a magical space, hidden in between the page of that book. Benjamin had wondered who actually wrote the book, for there was no mention of an author, only a publisher and the date the book had been published. Had many copies been published or only one? And if only one, this, to antiquarian book collectors, made it very rare indeed. Perhaps it had been made for a prince, a maharaja, one who lived in Arabia or India, both very magical places, and spaces where magic really was a part of the fabric of the land, the buildings and in the very air itself. No wonder magicians travelled to these two magical lands, for once they breathed in the air, they imagined they too would be able to perform miracles. At least they would with the magic rings illusion, also known as miracle rings.

Benjamin had always been good at maths although he was finding it hard to figure out just how this world of magic worked; at times it worked like a dream while at other times, well, the last thing he wanted to do was mention the N word (nightmare!) for fearing of bringing one down on his head. The night fell, thankfully not on Benjamin's head, as he wandered back along Abracadabra Street towards Matilda's Magic Shop where Matilda was waiting for him with a drink of hot chocolate. Had Benjamin imagined the whole thing? Had he been daydreaming as was his wont whether he liked it or not? No, Benjamin was certain a 1000.1% certain this had all been real; he could not explain it other than to place it under the giant umbrella (which wasn't pink but black) of MAGIC.

Benjamin couldn't wait to enter the world of dreams. He was so tired – magic wore you out; it was time to recharge his batteries. One thing he had learnt on his first day on Abracadabra Street was that he must be more street wise, watch his back, try and stay on the right side of Abracadabra Street and not under this street. Houdini might have perfected the Buried Alive illusion but the Worlds' Worst Magician, Benjamin H. Blackstone, H for hopeless, hadn't a ghost of a chance of pulling this trick off, unless he attempted it in the spirit world!

'Sorry,' grunted Benjamin, not looking where he was going as a magic carpet nearly knocked him into next week. He must remember he was living in a world turned upside down; he must stop walking around in a dream, daydreaming, staring at his shoes; surely this world was dream-like enough? He needed to keep his head up high, as his father and grandfather told him; when things went wrong, he needed to get back on the old metaphorical horse, or the old metaphorical stage, and the real one when you got booed off stage in the theatre. The same could be said of life, the theatre of life.

'Sorry? Not a bit of it, lad, I'm the one who should be saying sorry. I'm not much of a magic carpet rider, I'm more of a magic carpet maker,' the man sighed, stopping at the side of the street as if parking his magic carpet. *As this was Abracadabra Street, if there had been yellow lines outside the shops then no doubt the owner of the vehicles, horses, cars and magic carpets would have made them disappear*, thought Benjamin as once more the smile he'd been sporting after he left Matilda's Magic Shop returned.

'Is there a magic carpet race around these streets then?' Benjamin asked, putting two and two together, hoping in this world it still made four.

'Every Christmastime, as regular as clockwork, a part of the race takes place up there on Star Street,' the man smiled, pointing up at what Benjamin imagined was a painted starscape, unrealistic stars like giant diamonds painted a bright yellow colour for effect, like in children's storybooks.

'You have Christmas?' Benjamin exclaimed, looking more than a little bit surprised.

'Everywhere has Christmas, doesn't it? I realise you must be a stranger around here by all the questions, but surely, boy, you don't come from a place that doesn't have Christmas? I can't imagine such a place,' the bedraggled man replied, clearly wearing a carpet suit, and an old one at that. No doubt the carpet suit still contained some magic dust, in which case Benjamin should expect the man to take to the air and fly down the street with his magic carpet rolled up under his arms.

'No, I mean yes, yes of course we have Christmas where I come from... it's just...' Benjamin stuttered his reply then didn't know what he should be saying next, not wishing to give the game away. It seemed on Abracadabra Street, one wrong wish and you could either wish someone further or yourself. Benjamin had always imagined flying around the stars on a magic carpet; however, given his loathing of heights, in reality he had no wish to actually fulfil this wish. Wish-fulfilment was another modern expression in his world that he didn't care much for as, like the words 'amazed', 'unbelievable' and 'magic', it was used for every subject under the sun and more times than not was simply used for effect, like the glass ceiling. There was no glass ceiling in this world, only a cardboard ceiling, and one rainy day the roof of this world would collapse and that would be that!

One wrong word from Benjamin Blackstone, a word that was anything but magical, and this whole world could disappear, exactly like dark magic, and what was worse, it could take him with it. He may vanish for good or – crazy as it may seem – never have existed in the first place. Scientists in his world were always questioning the nature of reality; it was almost as if he was living in a popup world, a popup universe. There were popup shops, especially at Christmastime, popup radio stations, popup marketplaces, in fact it seemed Benjamin's whole world was built upon the idea that things were here today and gone tomorrow – more dark magic.

Never mind about this world being a façade, he was beginning to imagine his own world was a façade, a giant façade, a giant popup world. This wondering took Benjamin even further off the beaten track – what if his world had popped, or popped down, and the world he was now living in had popped up to replace it?

Benjamin felt as if his head was about to pop as he saw a million stars explode in front of his very eyes, eyes that felt as if they were about to pop out of his head at any moment. This most certainly did not qualify as a magic moment but it did qualify as a moment of sublime clarity. We create our own reality, more quantum magic from the wonder tellers of his world, the ones who told us the most unlikely tales of all time, that everything we see in the observable universe was conjured up out of a giant invisible wizard's brew.

Benjamin imagined it was he alone who was holding this world up, as if he was Atlas; he was creating the illusion using the magic of the mind, and it was true the mind was a very powerful tool. He mustn't give the game away, mustn't say the wrong thing; if he did, the trick, the illusion, would be spoiled and the whole of this world – Abracadabra Street and all – would disappear into thin air. Benjamin would then be no better than his great-grandfather Atticus Blackstone, who sold the family tricks, the Boy Who Sold the World, sold Abracadabra Street from underneath the feet of all those who lived and worked on this magical street, pulled the rug from underneath them. Or in this extraordinary case, the boy who took the magic away from a magical space, pulled the giant magic carpet from underneath them!

Benjamin loosened his imaginary bow tie for he was imagining he was rather underdressed to be performing magic on such a magical street, so he dressed himself up, at least in his mind, like a magician: ivory cane, silk black top hat and tails. It helped to look the part if you were a magician; the audience were more likely to believe you really could perform magic. 'I can't breathe,' Benjamin grunted, clearly having some kind of panic attack. Truth was, he felt claustrophobic, as if he was locked in a magic trunk inside an attic, both of which were full of dust. There was no air in this so-called magical space. Benjamin felt as if he would suffocate if somebody didn't let some air into… into the book… where was a giant child when you needed one? Clearly he was losing his mind… out of his mind… or so it must have appeared to those walking along the street.

'Magic, that's what it can do to some folk, they can't handle it, the magic takes over their mind, dark magic,' one magician sighed, shaking his head as he walked by on the other side of Abracadabra Street. 'Yes, best we walk on, don't get involved or they are liable to drag us down with them,' replied another magician, also not going over to see if he could help this poor unfortunate who clearly had a bad case of 'magic fever', a fever that had no cure.

The magic carpet maker could see Benjamin was lost, but he could not have imagined how lost Benjamin was; not just lost in the moment, he was lost in a world of his own, so many worlds of his own, it was as if he was attempting to spin plates on the end of a long pole – old-school variety entertainment. If one plate dropped it would cause a chain reaction and in the blinking of an eye, the ground would be covered in pieces of broken pottery.

'My name's Mr White, Oscar White to my friends, maker of magic carpets and part-time magician. My stage name is the Maharaja of Magic, terribly theatrical I know, but that's the magic game – it is terribly theatrical. I claim to work on the smallest but most magical stage of them all, a magic carpet,' proclaimed the man, hoping this would bring the boy back to the real world.

Benjamin didn't move, he just stared into space – what space was anybody's guess – one without stars, by the vacant look upon his face. Perhaps he had finally realised that, like the character in Hans Christian Andersen's fairy tale, 'The Emperor's New Clothes', he was as naked as the day he was born.

A giant shadow appeared on Abracadabra Street, overshadowing the street, the shops and all the characters upon the street. Amazingly enough, the shadow was of a child. She was sitting on the floor cutting out outfits made of paper, ones made for the characters from a popup book, or so Benjamin was now imagining, as another world popped up, then popped, disappearing back into his imagination. Some things you could dress up and some things you could not; in this world at this moment in time, Benjamin wasn't sure which was which.

It was as if Benjamin was now the only cardboard cut-out figure on the street, a street that, in his eyes, was anything but a magical one; it was a cobbled street in Victorian times covered with horse dung. And he was standing in a pile of horse dung so high it touched the imaginary sky. The man moved closer to Benjamin, took his hand and shook it firmly. This finally brought Benjamin back from his imaginary travels. Benjamin blew out his cheeks as if these travels had worn him to a frazzle, 'Pleased… pleased to meet you, Mr…'

'Mr White, Oscar,' the man added cheerfully and now it was Benjamin's turn to plaster a fake smile on his face.

'And the Oscar goes to Benjamin Blackstone for his outstanding portrayal of a man lost to time in the movie *Abracadabra Street*!' a voice cried out in a theatrical manner, a voice in Benjamin's head. Finally, Benjamin produced a smile worthy of a man with his feet under the carpet of a magical world, where anything and everything seemed possible, whereas in his small world, for him, nothing had seemed possible. That was the trouble with the modern world full of the fake and the plastic, a cynical world that even rubbed off on the young, taking the shine off old-school magic. Technological wizardry ruled the roost in Benjamin's world and he was not a technically minded person; technological wizardry, through Benjamin's eyes, was anything but magical. Thankfully, up until this moment, he had not bumped into a girl or a boy, head bowed playing with a technological gadget on Abracadabra Street. If that ever happened then, like in his world, the magic would disappear for him and all the good folk who practised their magic on this magical street.

As the years rolled by it took longer and longer for children to suspend their disbelief in both the real and the world of the storybook. But suspend one's disbelief Benjamin Blackstone must, if this illusion, this fantastical piece of magic, was to work!

'Time to suspend your disbelief, Benjamin my boy, and for the last time, there's no going back; it's time to live,' Benjamin muttered under his breath, mindful that he held this fragile little world in his hand and it would collapse around his ears like a house of cards if he did not handle it with care. Boy, was Benjamin Blackstone delusional; this world had been made in the Victorian era and half of London was built upon Victorian engineering. He had only popped up as if by magic into the modern world a small time ago and this world would probably still be going strong when he popped his clogs. And if he didn't keep his wits about him while he was daydreaming his life away, a man on a giant magic carpet would run into him as his clogs disappeared down a drain!

'Sorry, must be going, time flies, it's like being in a race trying to keep up with your competition to make sure your magic carpets are better than anyone else's. That's the trick, then you watch, they'll fly off the shelves of my magic shop as if by magic,' the carpet maker cried as he jumped back onto his old magic carpet and soon disappeared into his own shop at the end of the street. Benjamin had no idea how long the street was; it appeared to go on forever; perhaps it did, unless the street itself was an illusion like a giant magic circle?

'Goodbye and good luck; oh and I promise to pop in to your magic carpet shop sometime soon; I could do with a magic carpet!' cried Benjamin, waving to the man as he vanished from sight.

Suddenly, a shadow appeared by Benjamin's side as the sun disappeared, covered by a dark cloud or the shadow of a man, one who appeared to be permanently under the weather. Benjamin could hear the voice of his grandfather in his head, 'Benjamin, if a dark cloud appears over your head, pretend it's a magic carpet, jump aboard and your blues will soon disappear like the early morning mist on a beautiful summer's day, the magic of nature.'

14

The Shadow Caster

The shadow soon made itself visible; it was the old man he had first met on the street, Mr Wizenbaum, aka the Tarot Card Conjurer, aka the Shadow Caster or Caster of a Thousand Shadows. Just like before, Mr Wizenbaum was holding up a Tarot Card but one bathed in shadows. It felt to Benjamin as if he was in a silent black and white film where the speech of the characters was shown on the side of the screen. The last time, the Tarot Card had been depicted as the Wheel of Fortune; Benjamin was convinced this time his luck wouldn't hold and the card Mr Wizenbaum was holding up would be the Wheel of Misfortune. Benjamin slowly opened his eyes; thankfully it wasn't an illustration of the Grim Reaper, the death card, but it still was a card he imagined that would make his fortune.

'The Trickster!' Benjamin exclaimed, not sure if he was the trickster or it was the man holding the card in his face, Mr Wizenbaum. 'Who is the trickster supposed to be?'

'That's not for me to tell you, boy, I'm only a conduit for the cards to work their magic; the cards tell you your future, I cannot, I'm not Nostradamus, more's the pity.' The man smiled, another one of his crooked smiles which, through Benjamin's eyes, appeared to be more crooked every time he smiled, or at least attempted to smile, for it seemed more like a grimace than a smile, a false smile, the sort of smile which was hard to believe was sincere. Mr Wizenbaum's gaze then turned to Matilda's Magic Shop then quickly returned to look Benjamin squarely in the eye.

Benjamin was beginning to wonder if this strange man was going to keep popping up as if by magic – dark magic; he was also wondering if the man had a wandering eye, or perhaps a glass eye. The next time, this wizened-looking man might well be holding the Death Card in his hand, a card which had his name on it. Benjamin Blackstone – Dead from the Neck Up – The World's Worst Magician – may he rest in peace. The writing on this imaginary Tarot Card was clearly written in a fairy hand!

Benjamin as yet hadn't had time to read Arthur Edward Waite's book *The Pictorial Key to the Tarot* published in 1909 illustrated by Pamela Coleman Smith, or *The Book of Ceremonial Magic* by the same author. Both books had presented themselves to him after looking around Madam Matilda's library on books of a magical nature. Benjamin had simply thought of the books and as he passed by the bookshelves; the books had slid out as if to say, 'I hope these were the books you wanted?' *The Pictorial Key to the Tarot* was supposed to be the definitive guide on all things Tarot, showing both the major symbols of the Tarot deck and the minor symbols, which not many people were familiar with. If he could gain the knowledge of the Tarot deck then perhaps he could keep one step ahead of the Tarot Card Conjurer?

15

The Mirror Magician

'Let me introduce you to your partner in crime, I mean your partner in our little magic act, a magic act I hope will take us all into the big time where the greatest magicians and conjurer practise their magic: the Magic Circle in London, another magic circle of sorts. Perhaps if our fortune holds we will be invited into the inner circle of the Magic Circle like all the truly great magicians,' exclaimed Matilda, her eyes shining brightly so it looked as if two beams of a magic lantern were shining onto the wall of the magic shop.

If Benjamin screwed up his eyes he would see himself and his new partner working their magic on the greatest stage of all, the theatre of life. But was it Benjamin working the audience or was it his shadow, or perhaps a shadow puppeteer, a puppet master working both him and his partner? Another strange thought occurred to Benjamin as he saw a large looking glass on stage in his mind's eye but nobody in the audience appeared to see the looking glass; it was as if the mirror was somehow invisible. The looking glass reflected his personality and his image, a mirror image, but to the audience all they saw were two magicians working alongside one another, without the use of a beautiful assistant, a distraction to take the eye away from the trick that was being performed. The looking glass, a dark one, shattered halfway through the act and a magician covered in blood staggered out of the mirror and crawled across the stage, stopping in front of Benjamin.

Benjamin's mirror imaged clawed at his feet; he was trying to tell him something, desperately trying to get the words out as if to warn Benjamin of the hand he was about to be dealt. No doubt the hand was being dealt by the Tarot Card Conjurer standing in the shadows, waiting to upstage him and steal the show. This dark image quickly vanished to be replaced by a vision of loveliness.

'My name's Scarlet,' the young lady said in a whisper that felt like music to Benjamin's ears as her velvet voice entered the labyrinth of his ears, soothing his clearly troubled mind. Benjamin had a mind for magic but perhaps, like his great-grandfather, the black sheep of the magic family, it too was dark, as dark as the Black Forest, not an enchanted forest but a disenchanted forest, full of the darkest creatures imaginable.

'Delighted to make your acquaintance, my dear,' said Benjamin, playing the part of the perfect gentleman as the mist of the mind cleared to be replaced by a magic mist, the flower love-in-the-mist, for standing before him was an English rose. Benjamin bent over and kissed the gloved hand of the girl. Benjamin had imagined Scarlet was Madam Matilda's daughter although she had given no indication that this was a fact. The more likely story was it was a fictional one, conjured out of the mind of the World's Worst Magician, Benjamin Blackstone. Benjamin had also imagined Madam Matilda was from the royal bloodline of a Hungarian royal family and given the fact he was trapped in a Victorian book that his great-grandfather had found in an old bookshop in Hungary, then this made some strange kind of sense.

As long as Madam Matilda wasn't related to the "Blood Countess" Elizabeth Báthory, who bathed in the blood of the victims after she had tortured them to death, then everything was coming up roses. Those red roses would transform into black roses if Scarlet turned out to be a scarlet woman. Many great men of magic appeared to be tortured souls turning to the dark arts, unable to cope with the gift they had been both blessed and cursed with. Female magicians were so rare, Benjamin had no idea if female magicians suffered the same inner turmoil as their male counterparts.

Madam Matilda surely was too beautiful to suffer from the slings and arrows of outrageous misfortune. She smiled sweetly as Scarlet curtsied in front of Benjamin, as Matilda had taught her to do. Scarlet was playing the part of the perfect young lady. *Did perfect young ladies enter into circles where magic was practised, especially dark or black magic?* Benjamin wondered. 'Only if they practised black magic devil worship,' came back the rhetorical reply as Benjamin's smile turned into a grimace. Everything seemed to perfect, somehow; he was a stranger in a strange magical land and he couldn't perform magic for toffees, yet already he was being welcomed into Matilda's Inner Magic Circle being introduced to the greatest magicians of all time.

Yes it did appear all too good to be true but then again perhaps his luck really was changing; he was a changing young man. Why was he questioning his good fortune? Never look a gift horse in the mouth unless it belongs to a Trojan who specialises in giant acts of magic!

'Are you all right, Benjamin?' Matilda asked thoughtfully.

'Bothersome tooth, you couldn't make the pain disappear could you?' smiled Benjamin, turning the grimace on its head.

'No but I could make the tooth disappear; there is a magician on the other side of the street who owns a magic shop; he'll have that tooth out before you know it,' Matilda smiled. Benjamin imagined the dentist had already taken the tooth out before he knew it was bothersome, such was the magic the magicians on Abracadabra Street possessed. That was funny, the pain had gone, disappeared as if by magic; it was the oldest trick in the book – mind over matter.

'I'll let you two young people get better acquainted; you can look through my vast library of books on magic, see if anything jumps out at you, hopefully not literally, although I cannot make any promises. Last year an owner of a rival magic shop planted firecrackers in one of my books entitled *The Magic of Fire*. The book ignited when the book was open!' Matilda grimaced. Benjamin wasn't sure if Matilda had said this in jest to put him and Miss Scarlet at ease; if she had, her stage patter needed some work!

Scarlet giggled and her smile alone put Benjamin at ease for it appeared to light up the whole room. Benjamin wondered if this was yet another trick or once again if it was the magic of the mind working overtime? A smile was indeed a magical thing, a gift. Benjamin had to wonder why so many people walked around in his world with long faces. Another thing entered Benjamin's head, which was Matilda had cast a love spell over him and his new partner for love was indeed a most powerful magic. Love could lift you up so you felt as if you really were riding upon a magic carpet. Those lucky enough to be in love felt as if they could do anything, and what Matilda needed from her two protégés was just that self-belief. Benjamin smiled on the inside at the sheer idea, a ludicrous notion, preposterous in fact and one he instantly dismissed out of hand.

'I can't believe Matilda has so many books on magic; the shop doesn't appear that large, yet every time I walk to the end of the bookshelf another one appears exactly like—' said Benjamin. Scarlet finished off the line as laughter filled the magic shop, 'Magic!' Benjamin believed Scarlet had the magic touch for she touched the sleeve of his arm and a surge of electricity pulsated around his whole body. He had never felt so alive and in a world that had died years ago, the Victorian society. Benjamin had once read a fact that sounded like a fiction, which was that in Victorian London a society was set up to help those unfortunate troubled souls suffering from madness; it was called the Friends of Lunatics Society. Some things you could make up and some things you could not!

'Magic is no laughing matter,' sniffed Matilda, waving a black handkerchief around as if it were a magic wand. Madam Matilda had appeared as if by magic as she now stood in between Benjamin and Scarlet, which rather spooked them both. At least it spooked Benjamin; Scarlet didn't seem that surprised, almost as if she was expecting Madam Matilda to appear out of thin air.

'S... sorry,' Benjamin stuttered apologetically.

'Silly boy, I was only joking, nothing wrong with laughing, it helps to release the butterflies in the stomach, it's a form of magic,' laughed Matilda glancing up at a book on the shelf, and as she did, a stream of cream-coloured butterflies flew out of her mouth and disappeared out the door. This was not magic of the mind, this had actually happened, hadn't it? Benjamin wondered if the mushroom soup Madam Matilda had given him to satisfy his hunger pains had been made with magic mushrooms.

'Sorry, Benjamin, couldn't resist and I can't resist butterflies; they taste so good!' Matilda smiled, then did what no magician worth their salt should ever do: reveal how the trick was done. 'Cheap trick really, you see I am standing side on to you. A little distraction causing you to momentarily look up at the book of magic I had my eye on gave me the chance to open a box full of butterflies. I collected the butterflies from the meadow that is my back garden; I'm afraid my back garden is anything but magical. I really must get a gardener to cut the grass and pull out all the weeds.

'Now tomorrow, the real work will start so I suggest you both get a good night's sleep for we will be up at the crack of dawn to go through some rough ideas I have for a routine. Ideas are all well and good and often work like magic in the mind; however, they do not always work like magic when performed on stage. Our little act needs a gimmick. I'm always working on new tricks in the attic hoping the next trick, the next illusion, will be the big one. Up until now I've been disillusioned but I've a feeling, a good feeling, that together, as a team, the magic will work thrice fold, three being the magic number,' Matilda said, all smiles as she turned her back and once again disappeared.

16

The Magic of the Attic

'The attic,' muttered Benjamin almost in a trance-like state. The word 'attic' had always conjured up the magic for him and the last big magic moment happened in an attic. It probably was still working, one long magic moment that stretched way beyond the imagination although not beyond Imagination Street, for that street stretched even further.

'If our act doesn't work in an attic then it won't work anywhere; attics are the most magical of places; even if they seem anything but magical at first, the dust – nothing like fairy dust, just dust that makes one sneeze,' said Scarlet thoughtfully, also under the spell of the attic and attic magic.

'We both love attics, that's a good place to start,' Benjamin said, coming out of the trance this magical place had put him in.

'A great place to start, I would imagine,' Scarlet replied as a look of wonderment appeared in her eyes.

'A great place to start, I would imagine you are right,' Benjamin replied, mirroring the look of wonderment upon Scarlet's face as if these two young people were already on the same page of the book of magic.

'Where am I going to sleep?' Benjamin added, finally coming back down to earth.

'The attic,' Scarlet replied, almost as an afterthought.

'Where are you going to sleep?' Benjamin asked, feeling a little uncomfortable but he couldn't seem to stop the words coming out of his mouth.

'In the attic,' Scarlet replied, blushing a little.

'This is some magical magic shop; it has two attics!' Benjamin exclaimed, his eyes almost popping out of his head.

'No, Benjamin, you misunderstand me,' replied Scarlet, also feeling more than a little uncomfortable at the direction the conversation was heading in.

'I do,' Benjamin replied a little curtly.

'There is only one attic; we are both sleeping there but before you start to worry, remember this is a magic shop and all attics are magical, it may look small when you step into the attic but believe me I will be one side and you on the other. It will appear that we are so far apart, it will be as if you are on one side of the world and I on the other. We will need to step upon a magic carpet if we are to communicate with one another, there are rugs in the attic and carpets but I can assure you none of them are magical in any way whatsoever, so eaten by moths they would never fly in a million years.' Scarlet giggled as Benjamin breathed out a huge sigh of relief.

'Come on, dream land awaits and that land is full of magic both weird and wonderful,' Scarlet smiled, leading the way up the small metal spiral staircase that Benjamin was already imagining was made of glass, one that led to a star cloud. When Benjamin entered the attic he was more than a little surprised to see a washing line strung up between one side of the attic and the other, which divided the room. Hanging on that line were three carpets all of which Benjamin imagined were magic carpets, ones the dreamer only had to take off the line, place on the floor, step onto as they were whisked away onto Dream Street. This was a street holding a Night Bazaar, one being held under a golden full moon. The bazaar started in Constantinople, continued into Persia and ended in Timbuktu; this was a dream of a street for magicians and storytellers the world over.

Once you stepped onto this magical street, like Abracadabra Street, you never wanted to leave; it was a street where stories were told and retold. *The One Thousand and One Nights*, the original title of the Arabian Nights, literally flew off the market stalls as did the colourful magic carpets. The magic carpets appeared to know where the buyers of the carpet lived or so said the silver-tongued salesman as the carpet disappeared out of sight. Some said the carpets never arrived at the address they were supposed to arrive at, as once the buyer had moved on, the carpet came back to the stall they were being sold at. The Dream Tapestry in our heads was a most magical one, the threads arranging and rearranging themselves each and every night as the tapestry of dreams changed like a kaleidoscope before our very amazed eyes, eyes that were shut tight, yet the dream still managed to shine through like the beam of a magic lantern.

All dreams had to come to an end sometimes with a little help from a dark character with an even darker moniker, Mr Nightmare, who pulled the rug from under your feet, for this villain hated magic and hated magic carpet rides even more. Unless the dreamer fell into a nightmare, turned to dust and was never seen again in this world, as Dream Street vanished by dark magic. When this happened, however, in the world Benjamin now found himself in, there really was nothing to lose any sleep over for when he awoke and gazed down at the street below, Alacazam, Abracadabra, hey presto, there, laid out right before his eyes like a giant magic carpet would be Abracadabra Street.

It was true, the magic was inside your head all the time; it certainly was that way for one Master Benjamin Blackstone and Benjamin felt sure it was the same for Miss Scarlet Higgins, Miss and Mr Magic – now that wasn't a bad name for a magic act. It needed work, as did their act, or imaginary act at this moment in time. It was this double act that both Benjamin and Scarlet were already beginning to perfect in the Dream Theatre, where all their tricks worked like a dream. Of course the Dream Theatre had a false bottom, like most magic trunks, a false bottom which led to the accursed Nightmare Theatre where everything that could go wrong did go wrong.

Benjamin and Scarlet tossed and turned that long night, for they seemed to be on the same page of the Book of Dreams. The question was, were they really on the same page of the Book of Magic or was that too an illusion brought on by the magic spell of young love? Only time would tell what the truth was and what the illusion; for the meantime, Dream Time, everything was possible, nothing was off the table, a giant magic table where magicians from magic circles all over the world worked their magic. Scarlet and Benjamin felt overshadowed as if they were shrinking by the second and within the blinking of an eye they would disappear forever.

Benjamin was surprised he got a wink of sleep given the fact the steam wheels of his mind were churning like the wheels on a steamer on the Mighty Mississippi River. Where were his great-grandfathers, Atticus and Nathan? And if they had not sold the family magic secrets, then who had and why?

17

The Trick to Magic is?

'No, no that's not working either,' Matilda cried, almost tearing her hair out, for it was clear the magic wasn't working at this moment in time.

'I think we all need a break; come on, let's get out of this dusty space, it seems the magic and fairy dust isn't working its magic; perhaps the magic will reappear in the back garden. We can work in the summer house; we don't want anyone catching a glimpse of our act, although if anybody did I'm not sure they'd lose any sleep over our efforts,' Matilda sighed, looking glum.

'It's a lovely day,' Scarlet said, trying to make small talk with a boy who wasn't any better at small talk than she was; in truth, both Scarlet and Benjamin were better at stage patter than they were at conversing in the real world. Benjamin might not be any better at magic in this world than in his world, but at least his stage patter had improved under the watchful eye of Madam Matilda.

'Sorry about the garden,' said Matilda as the children fought their way towards the old summer house as if trekking through a jungle. Benjamin was surprised how big the garden was, given the fact all the houses on Abracadabra Street were close together with small gardens at the backs of the houses. It was that old black magic at work again, a small space becoming a large space when seen through the magic eye.

'Oh dear, sorry, Benjamin, I shouldn't laugh but that was funny,' Scarlet giggled as Benjamin tripped over his tongue then over his two left feet, ending up on his back with Scarlet staring down at him. 'You really don't have to fall at my feet.'

'I've got less control over my limbs than Pinocchio,' Benjamin said, sitting up like a puppet whose strings had been cut.

'Pinocchio the Italian puppet, which inspired Punch and Judy,' Scarlet said, turning the pages of a book entitled *The History of Vaudeville and Magic Acts* in her head.

'That gives me an idea; perhaps we could add some jokes into the act, lighten the mood then darken it before finally we let the light in, metaphorically speaking,' cried Matilda as the magic of the smile reappeared on her face.

'I'm naturally funny, or so my grandfather keeps telling me; I always thought he was joking, pulling my leg,' grunted Benjamin with a faint smile on his face. Scarlet helped Benjamin to his feet, brushing him down at the same time, 'Hey you're brushing away the magic dust. I dragged this jacket right along the entire length of the attic floor hoping it may rub off on me.'

'You better do a better job next time or better still, drag that jacket along Abracadabra Street, you might have more luck,' Scarlet replied with a straight face.

'Yes brilliant, bravo, bravo, more, more,' Matilda cried, enthusiastically clapping her hands and jumping up and down in a moment that the children thought was most out of character. Magicians for the most part tried to give off an air of mystery as if they had ice in their veins and nothing fazed them on or off stage.

Benjamin looked puzzled and so did Scarlet for they were not sure if Matilda was being serious or if she was being sarcastic; up until now she had not shown any trace of a mean streak. Perhaps she had been hiding it behind that magical smile. Benjamin decided Matilda was indeed happy at this slapstick routine and it was true all the magicians he had met so far on Abracadabra Street were deadly serious about their magic. He wondered how this light-hearted approach to magic would go down with the magicians in this world; were they ready for some light entertainment or would they all be thrown out of the magic circle? Benjamin had already entertained in his head that Abracadabra Street was a street designed on the Magic Circle emblem, a giant circular street.

Matilda could see her two protégés had chemistry between them and that using humour lightened the mood, a dark one up until that moment in time, and loosened them up; that was the trouble, they were too uptight. Matilda blamed herself; these were two young people, not experienced magicians; she was working them as if they had been on stage all their lives; no wonder the magic wasn't working. But now for one magical moment the magic had worked; it had come and gone in the blinking of an eye but it was there, a glimmer, if they could recapture that magic and the chemistry on stage then they may actually have something to offer the magic world, something different. Whether Abracadabra Street was ready for something different, well, once again only time would tell, for there had to be more than a few jokes and pratfalls if their act was to dazzle, astound and amaze this world of fantastical magic.

'We'll start the act with tricks that go wrong, make a joke of it, funny jokes, they must be good, then slowly the act will change, so through a metamorphosis from light-hearted to a more serious mood. I just need to find a trick and illusion that will knock people's socks off and more besides,' mused Matilda with a faraway look in her eye. 'The question is, where to find this fantastical illusion? Perhaps it will pop up as if by magic out of my head or perhaps it will pop up elsewhere,' said Matilda for she knew everybody could learn from somebody else, whoever that somebody else was, however young or old. Not to learn from others was, in Matilda's book, missing a trick. And you never wanted to miss a trick if you could help it, otherwise somebody else would steal that trick from right under your very nose.

'What if one of you wore a magician's outfit that was too tight, too short, while the other one wore a magician's outfit that was too big and baggy. You turn to Benjamin, Scarlet, and say, "I think you're shrinking and fast," to which Benjamin replies, "It's not me that's shrinking, this is a magic suit," to which you reply, Scarlet, "Not if it's by the same tailor that made the *Emperor's New Clothes*," referring to Hans Christian Andersen's fairy tale, of course. And then we need to get a good tailor who also makes magic tricks to make us two magical suits or at least one that appears magical or should I say more magical than your run-of-the-mill magician's outfit,' exclaimed Matilda as her mind exploded with ideas for her magic act. 'Laughter is indeed the best medicine for all that ails you; it is a form of magic.'

Benjamin of course immediately thought of the double act half-English Stan Laurel and half-American Oliver Hardy, Laurel and Hardy, Hardy wore the tight suit two sizes too small for him and Laurel played a ventriloquist's dummy to a mad tea party.

Benjamin hadn't realised Matilda had such a sense of fun; when he first met her he imagined she was a very serious woman until he was bedazzled by her magical smile, the same magical smile Scarlet had. Benjamin didn't want to ask but he wondered if Scarlet was Matilda's daughter; you would have thought she would have mentioned this little big fact. The reason might be a rather obvious one – that there was no husband in sight, and this was a time of the Victorians who some said were a rather prudish bunch by all accounts. Others said this was poppycock and the Victorian could throw as good a party as anybody else, certainly one to match the Edwardians, known for throwing big bashes especially during the roaring twenties.

A giant street party on Abracadabra Street, which could not possibly fail to deliver in the magic department, or so Benjamin was now imagining, an imagining he shared with Scarlet.

'A street party!' cheered Benjamin and Scarlet as one voice, throwing their imaginary party hats in the air , as they say, two heads are better than one, three even better although that would be the sort of dark magic often associated with Victorian travelling freak shows and stories involving witches and wizards.

'I like it; we could ask everybody to dress up and we could provide the entertainment or at least top the bill, certainly better than being bottom of the bill,' Matilda smiled then as another thought entered her head, not as magical as the last, the smile turned to a grimace. 'Well that's enough for one morning; I've got to open up my magic shop; I've left Mr Wilkins the old bookkeeper in charge, which probably means he's fallen asleep on the counter and there's a queue outside my shop that stretches from here to Timbuktu.'

'Come on, Benjamin, I'll show you around Abracadabra Street,' Scarlet said. linking her arm around Benjamin's as if they were a couple and were about to 'step out', as they say in old novellas where life was hard and romance even harder to find.

'Have we got time?' asked Benjamin, believing this street magical as it was stretched as far, further than the eye could see, even the Third Eye, a magical eye in the mind which sees things the eyes could not see.

'I imagine we have all the time in the world. I imagine we will be trapped in this magic moment for as long as we wish, Benjamin,' giggled Scarlet as if already walking upon a cloud with both a gold and a silver lining.

'Trapped in a magic lantern slide,' mused Benjamin adding to the short but magical tale the two children were conjuring up between them; by the time they had finished this tour around Abracadabra Street, Benjamin imagined they would have written a book together, a most magical book appropriately named *Abracadabra Street*. Scarlet was imagining the same thing, well almost; she was imagining Benjamin had written most of the story with her help of course and she had illustrated the book. Scarlet was quite the artist, her pavement paintings on Abracadabra Street were the talk of the town. Town, what town? Benjamin hadn't seen a town, he had only seen a street, both in this world and when he had opened the book in the attic. That extraordinary happening seemed a lifetime ago at this moment in time, if time even existed in this world.

Benjamin had imagined there were side streets to this small but gigantic street but he had never once imagined there would be a town; if there was a town surely it must be the town of Abracadabra. Wow, what a town this must be, the most magical town in the whole wide world, even if that world was trapped inside an old Victorian popup book. Forget

Constantinople, forget Timbuktu, forget Toy Town, they were small time compared to the magical town of Abracadabra where all magical moments were big time. Benjamin had heard of popup shops, popup radio stations even popup markets, but he had never heard of a popup town.

18

Popup Magic

'Are we going to town?' enquired Benjamin as he finally stopped imagining the town, for he was beginning to think it only existed in his imagination; yes, it was probably just down the road on Imagination Street.

'Yes we are,' Scarlet cried, quickening her pace.

'I wasn't sure if there was a town,' added Benjamin, his heart feeling as light as a magic carpet made out of invisible threads, as if the town of Abracadabra had just popped up out of the street as if by magic. It appeared Master Benjamin Blackstone, previously Jack of all trades, master of none, had the magic touch after all. But not as a magician, as a storyteller, as he gave Hans Christian Andersen a run for his money. Hans Christen Andersen probably lived somewhere on this street or on the next street, Imagination Street, along with his friend Lewis Carroll, Jules Verne, H.G. Wells, all who had unimaginable imaginations, streets ahead of any other writers of their time, the times of the Victorians.

'A town – what an imagination you have, Benjamin, of course there isn't a town – just a street. Why would you need a town or a city when you've got the longest and most magical street in the world? There isn't any room for a town,' Scarlet laughed at such a ridiculous notion, as sticking a prosaic town on such a magical space would spoil everything. What on earth was her partner thinking? Perhaps they weren't on the same page after all; perhaps he was the sort of fellow who still thought the earth was flat. He was more than likely a member of the Flat Earth Society. In truth, Benjamin and Scarlet were on the same page of a Victorian popup book, for there was only one page and they were standing on it and furthermore, when the book was closed and laid down flat on, say, a cabinet of curiosity, this world would be as flat as a pancake.

The illustration of Abracadabra Street must have been painted by an artist who really did have the magic touch for this touch of genius had literally brought the street to life or so Benjamin was now imagining. Perhaps the artist had once stood on the same street as he was standing on now; if that was not a surreal thought, he did not know what was. Since he had first stepped onto the street, these surreal thoughts had become more and more frequent; at this rate he really may find himself one day living on the same street as some of the great magicians, storytellers and imaginers of all time. Were these three professions not one and the same? Were magicians not also storytellers and storytellers magicians, ones with the most inventive and imaginative of minds?

'We're going shopping, aren't we?' sighed Benjamin, finally cracking the female code, the one he should have cracked a lot earlier, for his mother and two sisters were often going to town spending money like it was water in London town, a town where all the most expensive shops in England sat, not quite as magical as Abracadabra Street, but to his sisters and mother, it probably gave Abracadabra Street a run for its money. Benjamin tried to crack a smile but it just wouldn't come. *So much for magic*, thought Benjamin as he was brought back down to earth with a bump.

'You're a funny boy, Benjamin, and I mean that as a compliment; at this rate we'll be the talk of Abracadabra Street,' Scarlet smiled as her eyes lit up just like the beams of a magic lantern as, arm in arm, Benjamin and Scarlet went window-shopping along the street. And as they did, their eyes got brighter and wider with each shop they passed. Benjamin didn't know how many magical shops he had passed; he'd stopped counting after 150, and they'd hardly got more than a few hundred yards down the street. This, Benjamin knew, was a fact and not a far-fetched fiction, for he could still see Matilda's Magic Shop from where they had stopped for a rest. That was before Scarlet suggested they had better turn back before it got dark and the money in her purse ran out. Of course, Scarlet had no purse, for there was no need for money when you were just window-shopping.

Benjamin had a map of all his favourite magic shops in the world but they were not the magic shops, stores and emporiums on Abracadabra Street, they were the ones in his world. The list was quite long although some of the shops, due to the modern world, may have disappeared by now, as if dark magic was at work. The map and list was as follows, as Benjamin stepped onto his imaginary magic carpet and gave Scarlet a quick tour of the magic shops in his world: Davenport Magic in London; Joker Magic in Budapest, Hungary, a shop he was sure his great-grandfather had frequented – perhaps this was the shop that sold him the Victorian popup book,

Abracadabra Street; Haines House of Cards, Norwood, Ohio; Magic Land, Tokyo, Japan; The Magic Shop, Cape Town, South Africa; Tin City Magic, Naples, Italy; Ash Magic Shop, Chicago, Illinois; El Rei de la Màgia, Barcelona, Spain; Best Magic, Anaheim, California; and there were more, for Benjamin, being the living embodiment of the Magic Robot, could easily have performed on stage as a Memory Man.

Benjamin suddenly felt a tingle down his spine as he stepped off his imaginary magic carpet, offered his hand like a gentleman to his imaginary passenger, Scarlet, as they both stepped back onto Abracadabra Street.

Benjamin wasn't sure why or what, but something was telling him he needed to walk a little further down the street and as he did, he found himself walking down a small side street. The street was a little dark, or so he thought at the time, but not so dark it made him want to turn back.

In a moment, one Benjamin felt in some way was one that was about to get even more magical, a shop popped up before him as if by magic; it did not look that magical, which therefore meant inside it must be the most magical shop ever. Perhaps it was fate, written this way; Benjamin smiled, then another chill ran down his spine before running up it, for he could see a man in the shop window, and behind him, a man he recognised, and he had a pack of cards in his hands. What's more, the man, little more than a shadow, was shuffling the cards with one hand; these were not ordinary playing cards, these were extraordinary cards, not to be played with by those who did not understand the way life, the universe and everything in between work. The cards were Tarot Cards, which meant the shadow belonged to Mr Wizenbaum, who obviously had been following him the whole time.

This strange fellow, who hated wizards and appeared to delight in spooking the living daylights out of young lads, appeared to be his second shadow and one he could not shake off. Keep your friends close and your enemies closer; he should wave to Mr Wizenbaum ask him how he'd been since they had last bumped into one another. After all, they had a lot in common, they both disliked wizards with a passion.

'Come on, I want to go into at least one of these magical shops; I promise I won't buy anything,' grunted Benjamin, almost dragging Scarlet into the shop as if she were a giant rag doll. The shop now became more of a safe haven than a shop which performed magic; it was, after all, a bookshop, which sold books on the subject of magic and therefore at least the books on the shelves should conjure up magic on the written page. Benjamin had been looking for the book *Principia Mathematica* written by Sir Isaac Newton, said to be the last magician and a man who genuinely believed in alchemy, undoubtedly a form of magic, both light and dark.

'These shops are magical, so magical they will make you spend your money whether you want to or not,' Scarlet chided, trying to stop Benjamin reaching into his deep pockets as if under the spell of the shop, as he produced gold coin after gold coin, as if he really was a magician.

Where had Benjamin heard that line before? Oh yes, that's right, he'd heard it the few times he and his father had been out window-shopping with his mother and his two sisters!

'I have an iron will,' grunted Benjamin, lying through his teeth, teeth he imagined were now as crooked as Mr Wizenbaum's who, Benjamin imagined, was already in the shop before he had even entered through the door. At least his shadow was in the shop, for Mr Wizenbaum was still standing outside the shop window shuffling the cards, about to hold one up so Benjamin could see his future. Benjamin tried not to imagine this future; was he to buy the magic shop then run it into the ground to go bankrupt, only to find himself in the poorhouse, the workhouse, as he saw a giant house of Tarot Cards collapse on top of him? And there was the Grim Reaper laughing in his face, or at least the card was at the bottom of the pack.

Benjamin had never had much experience of laughing death in the face and black humour wasn't really his cup of tea, that was apart from the few times his father had forced him on stage to perform magic. It was there on stage that he saw his life flash before his eyes as Tarot Cards flew all around him so he was literally able to see his future right there in front of him. And it was funny how the Death Card, with the depiction of the Grim Reaper on the card, seemed to be the one that caught his eye before the cards disappeared back into the cabinet of curiosity in his troubled mind.

'Books!' Benjamin exclaimed as if he had never seen a book before in his life.

'Y… yes,' said Scarlet hesitantly, wondering if Benjamin was even stranger than she had at first imagined him to be. 'This is a bookshop; it sells books on magic; it rather does what it says on the—' Scarlet added, pointing to a sign on the wall of the shop.

'Tin!' Benjamin cried, trying to make a joke, a joke which rather went right over Miss Scarlet's pretty little head.

'A tin book? What sort of world do you live in, Benjamin? Sometimes I wonder,' Scarlet frowned.

'You'd never believe me if I told you,' grunted Benjamin under his breath then added over his voice as a smile appeared on his face, 'a most magical world indeed.'

'Good answer,' replied Scarlet, mirroring Benjamin, and as the two were now standing in front of a mirror, this line actually made sense. Benjamin looked in the mirror then looked into the mirror of the shop window as Mr Wizenbaum held up a card. Benjamin immediately shut his eyes muttering, 'What wizardry is this? I have no desire to be a wizard!' This made no sense to anybody but Benjamin, and those who had read the magical stories of… of… of who? Who had written these magical stories about wizards? Benjamin could not recall.

It was as if his world, the one he popped out of twelve years ago, was beginning to fade, as was his memory of his world. His world was Scarlet's world, his world was the world of Abracadabra Street, and soon his old world would vanish as if by dark magic and he would never see it or anybody he knew ever again. Benjamin wanted to share his secret with Scarlet but was afraid she would not believe a single word of it; even he didn't believe a single word of it and he knew it was a true story. Or was it perhaps he had been born in this world and he really was as mad as all the members of the Mad Hatter's Society put together?

This bizarre and surreal thought passed across the event horizon in Benjamin's head faster than a shooting star, faster than a steamboat named the Comet, faster than a comet in the heavens above, even faster than the speed of light. In theory, it was not possible, as Benjamin returned to the world that was around him, the world he could see, hear, smell and touch. What was real? What was reality? The grass was not green, the sky was not blue, it was a façade, no more real than this world was. It was as if a giant had simply painted his world so it looked like a giant stage prop in a Victorian or Edwardian theatre. It was Benjamin's sixth sense which was now working overtime to keep this world from folding up around him like a badly made house of cards.

This was yet another surreal thought to add to all the others; at this rate he would soon have enough to write a book, but one nobody would ever want to read in a million years! The Surrealist Movement had first appeared on the scene back in 1924 except the scene he was now starring in was back in the times of the Victorians. It felt to Benjamin as if he was reading this popup book while sitting on a chair with his back to a looking glass, reading the book from back to front; at this rate he could well find himself back in the times of King Arthur and the Knights of the Round Table. And if this was a fact and not a fiction, Merlin the Magician would be waiting for him to show him a trick or three.

Benjamin felt as if he was having an out-of-body experience as he turned on his heels so he didn't have to see the Tarot Card Mr Wizenbaum was holding in his hand. He half expected the man's shadow to pop up out of thin air holding the card so that he had no other choice but to see his future. Finally, he opened his eyes and he was standing in front of a bookcase with a book in his hands. 'I ley presto!' cried Benjamin, a cry he managed to stifle under his breath, for much to his surprise and amazement (and given the fact Benjamin had been surprised and amazed more times since he'd stepped onto this magical street than he'd ever been in his entire twelve years in his world), that was saying something.

However, Benjamin wasn't saying something, he wasn't saying anything, he was too dumfounded, too stunned to speak, he felt like a ventriloquist's dummy trapped in an old battered brown suitcase covered in labels from its travels all around the world.

'Benjamin, are you all right? It looks as if you've seen a ghost,' asked Scarlet resting her arm upon Benjamin's shoulder.

19

Ghost of a Chance

In a way, Benjamin had seen a ghost, or at least the book he was gripping onto for grim death surely must be a horror story, a ghost story by the look on Benjamin's face. The more likely story was the book was haunted, possessed by evil spirits or at least one evil spirit, as the face of his great-grandfather Atticus Blackstone appeared on the cover of the book, laughing in a manic fashion. The face disappeared but the haunted look upon Benjamin's face would take a little while before it disappeared. Hold on a minute, had he forgotten the story Merlin the Magician had told him? That's if he really was Merlin the Magician and a story it may well have been.

'Do you want to buy the book?' Scarlet asked, looking at Benjamin who didn't quite seem himself; in fact, he didn't seem 'all there', as if he was half in one world, half in another. The old 'Sawing the Lady in Half' routine or, in this extraordinary case, the new 'Sawing the Two Worlds in Half' routine, a waking nightmare, came into and out of Benjamin's troubled mind. It felt to Benjamin as if two phantasmagorical magic lanterns were operating in his head at the same time producing moving pictures. This thought may well have been inspired by the magic shop called The Magic Lantern, which sold all things pertaining to the lantern, which included thousands of lantern lithograph slides, all painted as if by a fairy hand. Scarlet had told Benjamin she had even painted some magic lantern slides, one or two of the street itself.

'Good choice; this is a most magical story,' the proprietor of the bookshop cried, for once not appearing out of thin air as if by magic but from behind the bookcase. Scarlet had heard this patter a thousand times before; she was certain the proprietor had used this line every time someone picked out a book from the shelf.

'We'll take it, charge it to Miss Matilda Moldova,' said Scarlet in a firm but polite manner, simply because she felt she needed to be elsewhere. Benjamin wished he was elsewhere, but that was simply wishful thinking on his part.

'Very well, madam,' replied the owner of the antiquarian bookshop, trying to prise the book out of Benjamin's hand without success.

'Don't bother to wrap it, I will take it as it is. I think you were right, the book is clearly magical as my friend has already been sucked into the book; his body is here but his mind is elsewhere.' Scarlet smiled, as did the owner of the bookshop. It seemed Benjamin was the only one who was not smiling. Scarlet took Benjamin by the arm still holding onto the book as they left the shop. Mr Wizenbaum was now nowhere to be seen; he had vanished, taking his shadow with him. Unless of course Mr Wizenbaum had taken Benjamin's shadow and replaced it with his!

Benjamin was not imagining such a thing; he wasn't imagining anything, he was still in a state of shock. Scarlet couldn't understand why, she hadn't even seen the title of the book as Benjamin's right hand was obscuring it. The book in her eyes looked nothing special, although the illustration on the cover looked rather striking; in fact, it rather reminded her of the street she was now standing on. Apart from that, no, the book was nothing special, it was like a million other books. Just because a book had the word 'magic' in the title or the book was a book on magic, it did not make it a magical book in any sense of the word 'magic'.

'Abracadabra,' Benjamin repeated in mantra-like fashion all the way home, his eyes vacant like an idiot savant, one who could see what others around him could not.

'You'll wear the magic out, Benjamin, or in this case the magic word; by the time you've finished it will no longer be considered a magic word, or at least not in my book,' exclaimed Scarlet, for try as she might, she could not get any sense out of Benjamin; all he could do was stare into space and repeat the magic word, 'Abracadabra', over and over again. If a word was repeated enough times, it stopped making sense. In truth, to folk that were non magical, the word had never made sense, any more than 'Hey presto' or the words 'Open sesame'. As this world didn't make much sense, then a word not making sense didn't seem that important.

Benjamin felt as if he was trapped in a lantern slide, but this lantern slide was a glass prison, one he was trapped in; he was banging his fists furiously against the pane of the window but he could not break it and nobody appeared to be able to hear him. This was how he often felt in his world; it seemed, no matter what world Benjamin found himself in, he felt trapped.

It seemed to Scarlet that the space Benjamin was staring into was not a magical space, it was a space with nothing in it but darkness; it was indeed a dark matter and a dark secret that Benjamin was keeping. It was even clearer to Scarlet, who at times appeared to have a crystal ball in her head, that the secret Benjamin was keeping, he wasn't ready to share, not even with his magical partner, at least not at this moment in time. This was not one of those magic moments Benjamin wanted to capture in the lithographic slide of a magic lantern; this was a moment he wished had not happened. But you could not erase that moment, no matter how hard you tried. It was stamped indelibly in your mind like a negative of a photograph; only time could erase the moment.

20

Abracadabra!

'Abracadabra, abracadabra, abracadabra!' cried Benjamin in his sleep and with every time he spoke the word, his voice raised an octave. So loud were the cries, it woke Scarlet up and she was right across the other side of the room, a room divided by a washing line and three thick magic carpets.

'Benjamin, wake up, you're having a nightmare!' exclaimed Scarlet, shaking Benjamin out of the nightmare she was sure he was trapped in.

'It's not true, it can't be true, it must all have been a dream, a bad dream,' Benjamin said, babbling away like a lunatic, in which case perhaps he would be better to take off his pyjamas and dress in a more comfortable attire like a straightjacket. As he was clearly the straight-man in this comedy magic act, that actually made some kind of sense. It certainly made more sense than the nonsensical thoughts he was having both in and out of the dream world.

'What can't be true?' Scarlet asked, looking even more puzzled than before.

'The book; we need to destroy it, burn it, rip it to shreds, it will bring nothing but trouble; mark my words, it's cursed, cursed, I tell you!' Benjamin exclaimed, clearly still in the nightmare, or so Scarlet was imagining.

'It's just a book,' Scarlet said, sitting on the side of his bed, soothing Benjamin's furrowed brow, which was so furrowed it looked like a corrugated iron roof.

'I wish it was,' Benjamin replied, breathing heavily as if he had been chased by the devil himself in this nightmare, or a madman by the name of Wizenbaum or the Grim Reaper; same thing in Benjamin's book of nightmares.

'It's just a book on magic, isn't it? Or is it one of those occult books on black magic? Surely you're not imagining the book itself can do magic? This isn't some sort of children's book of fairy tales,' Scarlet laughed, trying to make her friend see how ridiculous these notions were, but she could also see how vivid and wild her friend's imagination was when it got up a good head of steam. The steam wheels of the mind could both propel things forward or propel things backwards, depending on what mood or fancy the imaginative mind took.

'Look, Scarlet, I need to tell you something, something I should have already told you, but you can't tell anybody else, not even Madam Matilda. You have to swear, swear on a Bible or at least the Bible of Magic,' grunted Benjamin, sitting up in bed bolt upright as if he really had been possessed by an evil spirit.

'Not even Madam Matilda? It must be quite a secret you've been keeping; you're not a wizard are you? Because I can't work with a wizard and I know Madam Matilda could and would not entertain the idea. Wizards are little more than street entertainers in her book; a poor man's magician, a party magician at that!' spat Scarlet as the devil climbed out of Benjamin and jumped into Scarlet, or so Benjamin was thinking, wishing he didn't have quite such a vivid imagination.

'Wash your mouth out with carbolic soap! A wizard? Certainly not! I don't know how you can even entertain such an idea, a wizard indeed!' huffed Benjamin, finally seeing the funny side of Abracadabra Street. 'Look,' Benjamin said in a whisper, looking all about the attic as if he was sure in this magical place the walls really did have ears and reported everything that went on in this magical space to Madam Matilda, 'I just want you to know, however crazy this sounds, it's true, every word of it, as true as I'm standing here.'

'Given the fact you're *lying* in bed, we're not exactly off to a flying start with this truth-telling business, are we now?' Scarlet replied. Benjamin was trying not to imagine the bed flying out of the attic window, doing a loop the loop and tipping him off as he fell onto the street below, a story which had anything but a magical ending to it.

Benjamin ignored the comment and went full steam ahead with the story, hardly drawing breath before breathlessly, he finally ran out of steam. For a brief but long moment, Scarlet looked like a rabbit caught in a car's headlights until a broad smile appeared on her face as she opened her mouth wide and filled the attic with laughter.

'I'm being serious,' Benjamin exclaimed, sure the Court of Dreams had a false bottom, a nightmare, a waking nightmare.

'Okay, I'll play along with your little story, Benjamin, so this old Victorian book…'

'New,' Benjamin piped up, trying to get the story in some sort of order from the disorder Scarlet imagined it to be in.

'Okay, so this new Victorian book,' Scarlet looked at Benjamin, sensing another interruption, 'this popup book… is magical in more ways than one.'

'A lot more ways than one!' Benjamin added before Scarlet jumped in.

'Look, you've already had your go at telling the story, now it's my turn to tell it and as I do, perhaps we can make more sense of it, because I feel it needs editing somewhat.'

'Sorry,' Benjamin replied, biting his tongue, 'trouble is I have always had too much imagination for my own good and everybody else's too, I would imagine.' Benjamin sighed, feeling as if he was an outcast in whatever world he popped up in.

'Now where was I? Where were you? Oh that's right, falling out of dream into a giant Victorian popup book in an attic in an entirely different place and space to the one you are in now,' Scarlet added, raising her eyebrows so high Benjamin imagined they were about to disappear over the top of her head, reappearing at the back of her head, so it appeared she had eyes in the back of her head, as the old expression went. It may well be a new expression in this world!

'When I told the story, it seemed more believable, but when you tell it, it… well… it sounds unbelievable,' Benjamin groaned, sounding as if he no longer believed his own story, a true story, or so he had led himself to believe.

'There you go, you made the whole thing up, half in a dream, half in a daydream, leaving out the nightmare for the moment, although if I had my way we'd leave it out forever.' Scarlet grimaced then grinned, once again seeing the funny side of a boy others may imagine was funny in the head, but not in a good way.

'Thing is, I don't think I did make it up, the story, that is. I think the whole thing from beginning to end is true, every word, my memory isn't as clear as it was when I first stepped onto the street, Abracadabra Street. But it's clear enough for me to know it's a true story, even though it sounds like the tallest tale ever told anywhere in any time, space or place, magical or otherwise,' sighed Benjamin, blowing out his cheeks as he tried not to imagine Hans Christian Andersen looking outraged at this slight on his storytelling genius.

'Where's the book now?' Scarlet asked, her face twitching as if she were a cat in a previous life, hopefully not in this one, otherwise that made her a witch!

'Under my pillow!' replied Benjamin. Scarlet clearly thought he was joking until he pulled the book from underneath his pillow. 'Hey presto!' Benjamin added sheepishly.

'That makes a change from the old 'tooth fairy' fairy tale. There, you see, you dreamed the whole story up, it popped out of a dream and after all, it is a popup book,' Scarlet smiled, but Benjamin wasn't smiling, he was scowling, and this made her nervous. Could it be he really was telling the truth? It was true, she was living on a magical street; the sign on the side of the street said as much: Abracadabra Street, it couldn't be any clearer. The street had street smarts, it was streetwise, it knew every trick in the book, literally, in the book *Abracadabra Street*. It could lift you up to the heavens or drag you down to street level, below street level perhaps, into the dark, smelly Victorian sewers where rats the size of giant cats lived.

How could she have missed this rather obvious fact which sounded remarkably like a fiction? The street was telling anyone who had half a brain, 'Hey look at me, forget all these so-called magical shops, forget all the magicians and wizards who live on the street, I'm the star of the show, me, Mr Abracadabra!' Scarlet imagined the street to cry out in a most theatrical fashion, as was becoming of its theatrical street name. Benjamin imagined a giant picking up the book, carrying it under his arms wherever they wanted, then placing the book down, then, after a little magic, a shrinking spell, they were able to step onto the street. And if the owner of the book was a magician, well then, they would be able to test themselves out on the street with the best magicians in the world.

'Right, let's see some magic,' Scarlet exclaimed, snatching the book out of Benjamin's hand and laying it down upon the floor as she sat cross-legged on the floor of the attic as Benjamin joined her.

'Are you talking to me, the book, or yourself?' Benjamin asked, looking a little puzzled, which in truth was better than looking a lot puzzled, as he had been when the book first popped out of thin air in the bookshop. That was before the puzzlement was replaced by a look of amazement, then a look of horror. Just how many times was this book going to pop up? Three times, of course, three being the magic number, which meant it would disappear then pop up one more time.

'I'm… I'm not sure,' said Scarlet hesitantly, as now it was her turn to wonder if they should be dabbling in things in which they ought not to be dabbling: magic of a dark variety. Madam Matilda appeared to have a taste for magic of a dark variety, but that was something up to this point in time she had kept well hidden.

Benjamin and Scarlet waited and they waited and they waited for the magic to happen. Benjamin felt it was another repeat performance, the one he had witnessed in the attic in his world. He was about to start the old slow-hand-clap routine; he had even entertained booing as if he had regressed to his childhood, as this was clearly a pantomime! If this book did contain an evil spirit, it seemed as if, at this moment in time, the book wasn't going to give up the ghost; another old-time saying. If it was, it wasn't going to give up that ghost and its secrets without a fight!

21

Small-Time Magic

'It takes a little time to warm up, a bit like a warm-up act supporting a famous magician or an old television set; oh sorry, the television hasn't been invented yet in this world. It's like a magic box, I'll tell you about it later,' Benjamin gabbled, the words spilling out of his mouth like water. The excitement grew, the longer they waited, until it grew so much it felt to the children as if they were going to explode or suffer a rare case of Victorian Spontaneous Human Combustion. There was nothing spontaneous about this magic act; the actors and, moreover, the stage manager and impresario who owned this small theatre of magic were certainly cranking up the tension and excitement to eleven. It certainly felt to Benjamin and Scarlet as if they were watching a magic act. Then, all of a sudden, exactly by magic, the book burst open as, spontaneously, Scarlet and Benjamin cried out in a loud voice, 'Abracadabra!'

Right there before the children's eyes, they were treated to a magic show like no other. The little magicians performed tricks and illusions that made the toes curls and the hair stand upon end like fairy sparks. Sparks literally flew out of the book as if there was an indoor fireworks display going on inside the book or on the street, Abracadabra Street. Scarlet and Benjamin were spellbound, entranced, amazed, all the magic words they could think of, some words they could not, for it was hard to describe just how magical this event, happening, show was.

The words which in Benjamin's head normally flowed like silver from a mercury fountain in a garden paradise in Persia (if not out of his mouth in such a free-flowing manner) became jumbled up. It felt to Benjamin as if a juggler was in his head juggling words he'd plucked out of a thesaurus as he sat there, eyes as wide as saucers, with an expression best described as 'wonderment', the old-fashioned word for wonder. This was old-fashioned magic at its very best, guaranteed to astound and amaze or your money back, although this show appeared to be free.

Then, with the finale in sight, or so Scarlet and Benjamin were both imagining, the show ended abruptly, as the door of the attic opened and in walked a shadow. Benjamin was the first to turn around, the spell broken, half imagining it was the Grim Reaper walking towards him or Mr Wizenbaum working the Grim Reaper like a puppeteer, or a shadow puppeteer in this extraordinary case.

There were many dirty tricks one could play on a person, but the dirtiest and cruellest trick of all was old age, Old Father Time, a dark magician indeed. Benjamin wondered if folk aged in this world, trapped in a book trapped in time.

Of course they did; even books aged, became dog-eared, smelt musty and the pages turned yellow, holes appeared in the pages caused by dust mites and moths and eventually over time they turned to dust, a pile of dust, perhaps magic dust in the case of Abracadabra Street. It was this dust a magician or conjurer may use to sprinkle over his magic act after which, hey presto, abracadabra, he became one of the greatest magicians of all time.

This was a story Benjamin had conjured up one day in the attic in his mind, for at the time he wasn't in a magical space, he was in a loft which had been converted into a bedroom.

It was neither of these dark characters, it was Madam Matilda dressed in black which, in the half light of the candles in the attic, made her appearance shadow-like.

'Children, it's way past your bedtime, we all have to get up early in the morning. I want to show you my new trick, I think you'll like it,' Matilda purred, a slight smile flickering across her face as the candles appeared to flicker, then go out, then relight themselves. It was probably the children's imagination, for at this moment they were seeing magic wherever they looked.

'I... I thought I saw that book close on its own... must be the poor light... that and my tired eyes... now come on, children, put the book away and get back to sleep,' Matilda cried, shooing the children across the room and into bed like a shepherd tending to their flock. She tucked the children tightly into bed, too tightly for Benjamin's liking, for now he felt as if he was wearing a straightjacket. Was that a wicked grin on Madam Matilda's face upon seeing the discomfort upon the children's faces, or was, once again, his imagination working overtime?

Madam Matilda blew out the candles then left the room with a look on her face of puzzlement and curiosity. She felt sure something had happened that night that would change all of their fortunes; it was a feeling, nothing more. Madam Matilda prided herself on her ability to see things and feel things that weren't there. Madam Matilda didn't however regard herself as a clairvoyant or a soothsayer, one who could see spirits or see the future, but she could feel the vibrations of the world around her, could read the signs without any help from the Tarot Cards.

In his world, Benjamin lived in a street with probably the most prosaic and down-to-earth street name in the world, for it was called 'The Street'. Yes, I know, it's hard to believe, but believe it you must, or at least suspend your disbelief until you leave Abracadabra Street!

22

Trick or Treat?

'Prepare to be astonished and amazed,' Matilda cried as she pulled off a giant black sheet that covered something very large.

To the children, it appeared as if she was performing her new trick in front of an audience, a small audience, it has to be said. How small that audience was, was hard to say, as the trick was being performed in the attic space, then very small, as if there were in fact fairies living in this small but magical space, as sometimes depicted in fairy stories. Benjamin wasn't sure if the magic was astonishing, certainly not amazing, unless what they were now looking at was an invisible maze or Hampton Court maze, which Madam Matilda had somehow moved from one magical space to another while moving it from one world to another at the same time.

'What are we supposed to be looking at?' Benjamin was the first to break rank, sounding not unlike one of the characters in the fairy tale *The Emperor's New Clothes*.

'Isn't it obvious? Perhaps it isn't. I'm no carpenter, I'm afraid, it's only a rough working model. Later I will employ a real craftsman to build it,' Matilda said, trying to put the wind back into her sails, the wind Benjamin had so cruelly taken out. A windmill in an attic – why ever not? No point skimping on the magic in a story where magic takes centre stage.

'It's… it's a giant book!' cried Scarlet, leaning to one side so she could see the illusion, the trick, in a better light although if all the audience had to perform contortions to see this piece of stage magic then that might prove problematical, thought Scarlet.

'Yes!' cried Matilda, now sailing on cloud nine in a boat named *Wishing on a Star*.

'How does the trick work?' Benjamin asked, beginning to fear the worst, but at least, as yet, the worse than worse had not happened, Charles Dickens' worst of times, thought Benjamin, hoping he was wrong and the best of times were just around the corner.

'The trick illusion works like this: Benjamin, you and Scarlet stand in the middle of the book then before the show starts the book folds up and you disappear from view. Don't worry, this isn't a twisted version of Sawing the Lady in Half. Then I open the curtains and perform the trick, or should I say I come on stage, give the audience the old magic patter, wave a large magic wand over the book and it opens and as it does you both cry out—'

'Abracadabra!' Benjamin and Scarlet cried out as one voice.

'Good, I'm glad we are all on the same page of the magic book, which I'm sure you have already worked out before is the popup book you were playing with a few days ago in the attic, you both being as bright as buttons,' Matilda added, as Benjamin took the opportunity to jump in.

'Leaving out Buttons from the pantomime *Cinderella*,' Benjamin quipped, turning to Scarlet who replied, 'Naturally,' to which Matilda added, 'My, have I taught you well? It won't be long before you're teaching me.'

It was then that a thought popped into Benjamin's head – had Matilda seen more in the attic than she had let on? Had she seen the little people pop up onto Abracadabra Street exactly like magic, or had the idea simply popped out of her head after seeing the Victorian popup book on the floor? Never mind about 'Pop Goes the Weasel', the old children's nursery rhyme, Benjamin felt as if his head was about to go pop. And if Benjamin was holding the whole world together simply using the magic of the mind, then Abracadabra Street would pop like a giant balloon. Furthermore, and that should have been more than enough regarding popping in this popup world, everybody on the street, magicians and wizards alike, would all pop their clogs at the same time, at least this would be the case for magicians and wizards who came from the Duchy of Holland!

Even if Madam Matilda had seen the miniature street magic act at work, and that was far from certain, this giant version of the book wasn't magical in any shape or form; it was contrived magic, real magic only works in the natural sense, organically. At least Benjamin thought so, as his inner voice got up a good head of steam. If Benjamin was not careful, steam would pour out of his ears like a kettle about to boil over, or a stream train that was on the verge of being derailed!

'If everybody would like to take up their positions, we will give the new act a run-through,' cried Matilda, cupping her hands as she took on the role of stage manager and actor manager in the small but magical Attic Theatre. Madam

Matilda had already given the theatre a name: Theatre of Magic. She had toyed with putting her own name before the word 'theatre' – Matilda's Theatre of Magic – but it sounded like a bit of a mouthful so she wisely decided to leave the name of the theatre as it was.

The rest of the day and that week were spent perfecting the act and all the while a carpenter and maker of magic illusions and tricks, Mr Banini, an Italian of many years' experience, set about constructing the full-size working model of the Victorian popup book. Mr Banini even painted the wooden covers of the giant popup book/illusion/trick the same colours as the original book, taken from a picture that Scarlet had painted. Matilda asked the children for the book so Mr Banini could reproduce the book as close to the original as possible. The children were horrified at the prospect of their secret getting out, especially Benjamin, so he told Matilda a white lie. 'The book appears to have disappeared as if by magic,' Benjamin told Matilda, lying through his teeth, which once again he imagined were as crooked as Mr Wizenbaum's crooked teeth. 'Well, after all, it is a magical book, or at least the title of the book gives that impression, another tall story.'

Scarlet smiled, not wishing to give the game away for she was about to say, 'Well, after all, it is a magical book, says so on the cover: *Abracadabra Street*.' Thankfully she did not, as Benjamin imagined if she had, the book would magically appear out of thin air right before their very eyes and the game would be up.

23

The Attic Theatre

'Children, I have invited a small but select group of people to come and watch our first show in the Attic Theatre a sort of run-through for the big day, the street party at the end of the month,' Matilda proclaimed, clearly practising her skills as master of ceremony, or mistress in this case. 'Don't take this as a slight against your skills as magicians, I just want to iron out all the little flaws of the act so it is as magical as it can be, perhaps not perfect, for flaws are a part of life and magic, and we don't want to take the magic out of magic.'

'When is opening night to be?' asked Scarlet as both she and Benjamin held their breaths; it was exciting to be a part of something, something big, but when the day or night came, when the dream became a reality, the butterflies started to fill your stomach then your throat, blocking the windpipe, making it feel as if you were suffocating or dying on stage!

'Tonight, I thought it was better if I kept you in the dark for as long as possible; that way there will be no time for last-minute nerves,' Matilda smiled as sweetly as she was able, crossing her fingers behind her back and wishing on every star, fake or otherwise, in the heavens above.

'We're… we're not ready,' cried open-mouthed Scarlet and Benjamin as one voice.

'An actor or magician never knows if they are ready until they go on stage or, moreover, know if they're ready until they come off stage; the audience will tell you if you're ready or not, there is no dress rehearsal for life,' Matilda replied, waving away all the children's reasons why they could not perform the act, the act which Madam Matilda was sure they were born to perform. The word 'REHEARSAL!' followed by an exclamation mark popped up out of Benjamin's fevered mind, as he removed the RE and the AL, which left the word 'HEARS'. Without the E, but it was as close as damn it to the worse 'HEARSE'. In Benjamin's mind's eye he had died on stage. Matilda had placed him in a magic trunk, a coffin of sorts, and then placed him in a glass funeral carriage to be pulled by four black mares. For a magician, being buried in a magic trunk, as long as you weren't alive, was a nice touch without the magic. Benjamin did not imagine for one moment he was Lazarus or Harry Houdini who had performed the 'Buried Alive' trick on more than one occasion.

'Don't worry, children, I have hand-picked the audience; they are all friends of mine. They all want you and me to succeed,' proclaimed Matilda, although something told the children this wasn't strictly true. Was she protecting them from the critics she had invited, hoping for great reviews, which would set them all up for life? Matilda hadn't looked them in the eye when she proclaimed this, and that, to the children, was a tell-tale sign that their mentor was telling tales. The question was, what sort of tales was Madam Matilda telling the children and how big were they? Benjamin was already worrying himself to death; what if his heroes Harry Houdini, Robert Houdin and Merlin the Magician were in the audience? He was sure to die on stage as they died laughing, more magic as black as the non-colour bone black.

There was really no time to think on the matter further; it would be all right on the night, as the old theatrical saying went, and if it wasn't all right on the night, well, there would always be another night, you just picked yourself up, dusted yourself down (making sure the next time you were on stage you were wearing an outfit covered in fairy or magic dust) and got back on the old imaginary horse, the stage, and if you were lucky and the magic was working, it felt as if you were flying on the back of Pegasus the Winged Horse, or perhaps it felt as if the theatre itself had grown wings and now you were performing on Star Street on the greatest most magical stage of them all.

The big night came and went in the blinking of an eye. Scarlet and Benjamin felt as if they were performing their small-time magic act in the Attic Theatre as if in a dream. Except in this dream their actions were anything but dream-like; in fact on stage, the children were like automata, their movements jerky. Benjamin imagined he was one of John Joseph Merlin's automatons. Despite this, the small audience appeared to love the act, cheering wildly. Benjamin wondered if Madam Matilda had paid the audience to cheer at the end of the act so as to give Benjamin and Scarlet the self-belief they clearly needed. Alternatively, Madam Matilda had cast a magic spell over the audience so through their eyes everything appeared to work like a dream, like clockwork, in fact.

Whatever the truth, it certainly did give Benjamin and Scarlet a much-needed lift, so much so, it made the children feel as if they really were walking on air. This meant there was no need for the children to jump on a magic carpet every time they needed to pop out to the shops, one of Madam Matilda's little jokes. In truth, on Abracadabra Street, there didn't appear to be any other shops than magic shops Benjamin had not seen a corner shop that sold food or a greengrocer's; it seemed everybody on this magical street ate, slept and breathed magic.

24

Street Magic

While all this was going on, other things were going on that were not necessarily of a magic nature; the street was getting a makeover whether it liked it or not. 'Oh, do I have to dress up for the occasion? I'm not a child anymore,' Abracadabra Street groaned after being told there was a street party planned for the weekend and, as such, the street would be dressed up to the nines and possible the tens as well.

'The party we are putting on is for you; it's your birthday, you're a hundred years old on Saturday. Queen Victoria and Prince Albert and all of their children will be there and all the Kings and Queens of Europe, princes, princesses, all the maharajas, emperors and empresses from around the globe, all looking to impress the greatest street in the world, Abracadabra Street. We simply must not disappoint them; we must put on the greatest show on earth, the greatest magical show on earth!' cried the Major of Abracadabra, the town that didn't exist.

Oh, the town of Abracadabra existed all right, it was just it was invisible; either that or made of the magical substance known as moonstone, pure moonstone, so it was impossible to see it. Until you bumped right into it or it popped up right in front of your very eyes as if by magic, perhaps exactly like magic. All the houses in the town of Abracadabra were box-shaped, like giant magicians' magic trunks. The magicians who owned and worked on Abracadabra Street also had a second property in the town of Abracadabra. This was a story Scarlet had told Benjamin one night when they were both unable to sleep due to the excitement of the upcoming event; whether it was true or not, Benjamin was not sure, but it certainly made him want to find out for himself.

Scarlet told Benjamin that only the most imaginative of minds and ones who possessed the ability to do real magic were able to see the town of Abracadabra. This story had Hans Christian Andersen's magic fingers written all over it, and it was true that Hans, despite being compared to a giant stork, did have magic hands, creating great paper art with little more than pinking shears.

Benjamin eventually drifted off to sleep and had a most magical dream; he found himself in an attic and in that attic there was a book – Victorian, naturally – a popup book without doubt. The title of the book was one word in bold black capital letters followed by an exclamation mark, simple and to the point, a title that might at a pinch of magic dust pop up and take your eye out if the book really was magical, that word naturally being: ABRACADABRA!

The book popped open, no big surprise there, and Benjamin was sucked into the book once again without wishing to spoil the story (no spoiler alert necessary), all very predictable. And what was wrong with that? After all, not all dreams had to be weird without the wonderful surreal nonsense that the dreamer could not make head nor tail of. There was nothing wrong with a story that popped up and did what it said on the cover, and nothing wrong with a dream that was simply a dream from beginning to end, very story-based, without a nightmare in sight or a trap door, a false bottom in that dream that led to a nightmare. It was plain sailing all the way; life is like a dream, as Benjamin found himself in a small little sailboat with Scarlet named Abracadabra, as they sailed their way around the town of Abracadabra clearly in somewhat of a dreamy state.

The night before the street party, Scarlet had a dream and in that dream she found herself on Easy Street dreaming of Abracadabra Street, hardly surprising given the fact she lived and worked on the street. Somehow, she found herself inside the mind of the street as if it was a living, breathing entity, which it may well have been given the fact some religions and cultures believed everything had a spirit or a soul. Even inanimate objects were said to have spirits, and there was nothing more inanimate than a street. If this had not been the case, streets would be flying here, there and everywhere like magic carpets; can you imagine the confusion that would cause?

A Victorian street would end up in Constantinople while the street in Constantinople would end up in Timbuktu or Persia! It just wouldn't do simply having one magical street named Abracadabra; this magical street would need to do a world tour at least once in a blue moon and, as we all know, magic is only magic when it happens once in a blue moon.

As Scarlet's surreal dream continued at pace, Abracadabra Street began to dream of a giant blue toy box which belonged to Pandora; the street appeared to know the toy box belonged to Pandora because it said so on the side of the box. The toy box was painted with colourful pictures of teddy bears, alphabet blocks 'A', 'B' and 'C', toy tricycles and dolls. Out of the toy box popped many different outfits including an outfit Alice in Wonderland would have been proud to be seen in (a nice little blue-and-white sailor's outfit) and one Little Lord Fauntleroy would have been equally proud to be seen in (blue velvet shorts with a top to match) as Alice and Lord Fauntleroy paraded down Abracadabra Street, arm in arm.

The street being magical as it was could dress itself up in a thousand different ways so it saw no reason to dip into a children's dressing-up box to find a suitable outfit for the street party to end all street parties. Abracadabra Street felt this was beneath it and given the fact the street could take to the air like a magic carpet, it really could fly over and under the rainbow and over and under the moon bow.

Abracadabra Street was able to transform itself from a street in Timbuktu to a street in Constantinople to a street in Persia back to a Victorian street in the blinking of an eye. Just one word from this magical street, the word of course being 'Abracadabra', and it was all change. The street party to end all street parties; was this to be the last street party on Abracadabra Street? Well, if the street really was a hundred years old, a grand old age in anyone's book, then it could well be the street's last birthday, so the good people of Abracadabra wanted this party to go with a bang.

25

The Maharaja of Magic

Benjamin found sleep hard to come by; he had so many butterflies in his stomach, tonight just might be the night he finally mastered the art of flying both in and out of your sleep. Fed up with staring at the ceiling of the attic counting imaginary stars, he threw off the sheet, put on his clothes and slipped out of the attic and into the street.

There was magic in the air in more ways than one as Benjamin was almost knocked into next week by a magic carpet; however, there was nobody on the carpet unless they were wearing a cloak of invisibility that the wizards wore to keep out of sight. There were hundreds of magic carpets flying this way and that, up and down the street, seemingly touting for business. *They are certainly given the hansom cab drivers a run for their money,* thought Benjamin, as a faint flicker of a smile appeared on his face. Benjamin glanced into one of the windows of the magic shops and couldn't resist saying in a loud voice, 'I'm so far through the looking glass, it's not true!'

'Magic carpet ride, mister?' a magic carpet cried, stopping in front of Benjamin a couple of feet off the ground. 'Best ride you'll get in these parts and only a penny farthing.' Upon the carpet was a flea-bitten carpet bag that looked anything but magical and a carpet beater, one Benjamin imagined he would beat himself up with, and as long as he did, he would retain the title of World's Worst Magician. Benjamin was sure this wasn't one of the magic carpets the Maharaja of Magic made, for when it came to makers of magic carpets, Mr Oscar White, aka the Maharaja of Magic, had the magic touch.

Benjamin put his hand in his pocket then delivered a line he thought somewhat amusing; perhaps he could use it in the act: 'Sorry, haven't got a penny farthing in my pocket, my pockets aren't that deep.' Benjamin waited for the laughter but got nothing but silence; obviously magic carpets weren't that bright or perhaps they simply didn't understand humour, or the more likely story was they were dead on their feet at the end of a long shift and couldn't be bothered with stupid boys who thought they were funnier than they really were.

'The World's Worst Magician, more like the World's Worst Street Entertainer. Sorry, boy, we don't barter over magic carpet rides, it's a penny farthing or I'll be on my way,' the magic carpet grunted, clearly tired of humouring this boy.

'Stick it on Madam Matilda's tab,' said Benjamin, pushing his luck, which was better than pushing a barrow around the streets of Victorian London or a broken-down flea-bitten magic carpet back to Persia, where Benjamin imagined it came from.

'Oh that's right, you're Madam Matilda's boy, sorry, didn't recognise you in the half-light, step aboard, I'll take you for the ride of your life,' the magic carpet said in an apologetic tone. The carpet lowered enough for Benjamin to step onto it but as he was about to, the carpet shot forward a few feet and Benjamin fell flat on his face.

'Slapstick; now that's what I call humour!' the magic carpet laughed almost splitting its sides as several threads came loose and fell onto the street. Benjamin imagined he had lost the thread of the Dream Tapestry some time ago.

'Okay, now we're even, step aboard Dreamer and your dreams will come true,' said the magic carpet in a dreamy monotone.

'Why can't I be like everybody else and meet a talking dragon?' sighed Benjamin as the magic carpet reversed and hovered a foot off the ground in front of him. Benjamin wondered if he was about to be taken for a ride but not in a good way. What if the carpet was possessed by the evil spirit of a wizard? Alternatively, the carpet might be possessed by a witch but which witch? A white witch, a practitioner of Pagan magic, white magic, or an old witch, a practitioner of the dark art, witchcraft?

Hesitantly, Benjamin stepped onto the carpet and *whoosh*, the carpet flew into the air, causing Benjamin to do a somersault. 'Wow, that was some trick!' cried Benjamin, as high as a kite.

'That's nothing, I'll show you moves that will make your toes curl and your hair stand on end like fairy sparks,' cried the carpet, higher than a kite.

'Not you, I was referring to my somersault; I've never done a somersault before in my life; perhaps we could include it in the act,' Benjamin beamed, bringing the magic carpet down as he did so for, as the words left his mouth, the carpet began to fall and fall and at such a speed Benjamin was now hanging on for dear life.

Then the carpet rolled. 'A death roll? What next, a death spiral?' exclaimed Benjamin as the carpet rolled and he was now upside down hanging on by a... you guessed it... by a thread! 'Is this the ripcord of the magic parachute?' spluttered Benjamin as he pulled the thread he was hanging onto and the magic carpet began to unravel before his very horrified eyes. 'Heeeeeelp!'

For a few moments, which were undoubtedly magical, Benjamin Blackstone was on Cloud 9 and had high hopes of climbing onto Cloud 99, a star cloud, but the threads of the Dream Tapestry were unravelling before his very eyes and not in a magical way! Sometimes the Dream Tapestry unwound then rewound stitch by stitch, stitching itself back together by the magic of the subconscious mind.

While Benjamin was having a nightmare, Scarlet was having a bad dream, a dream where her friend, colleague and fellow dreamer was trapped in a waking nightmare.

The ground was coming up fast; it looked like Benjamin's dream of flying had turned into a nightmare, a waking nightmare; then, as he closed his eyes fearing the very worst, (leaving out the very worse than worse!) he felt himself land upon a cushion of air. 'Thank god!' sighed Benjamin as he opened his eyes to see he was lying on nothing, unless this was an airbed; the more likely story was he was lying on an invisible magic carpet. 'Wizard!' cried Benjamin, unable to help himself. 'When I say "wizard", it's a word schoolboys used back in the 1950s, and after all, I am an old schoolboy,' babbled Benjamin, trying to get himself out of a black hole of his own making, for in his mind's eye he could see the Wheel of Misfortune.

This time, however, it was a different story entirely; the wizards with their pointy wands had been replaced by magicians; the wands weren't wizards' wands but stage props.

These stage props had been sharpened at the end so they were razor sharp and the magicians were all lined up ready to throw them at the Wheel of Misfortune, and moreover at a certain person who had changed sides overnight to become a wizard, a wizard of all things.

It was a nightmare all right, or it would be if Benjamin had been asleep in his bed instead of asleep on a carpet of air on a certain magical street, which guaranteed you a dreamless sleep or your money back.

Benjamin was fast asleep and snoring, so he didn't hear two voices whispering as the carpet flew through the window of the attic, trying not to pull the rug from underneath this dreamer as Benjamin finally came back down to earth and for once not with a bang but a whimper. Benjamin turned over in his sleep, sighed contentedly as if finally he'd learnt to fly like a... magic carpet.

'What a dreamer; that boy can dream for England.'

'He can dream for Abracadabra Street.'

'Keep your voice down, you'll wake up the whole street!'

'Not a chance, I'm such a great magician I can do magic in my sleep.'

'Big deal, I can do magic standing on my head.'

'So you can, very impressive, I must say.'

Now either two magicians were keeping an eye on the boy who lived... in a world of his own... or two magic carpets had taken pity on Benjamin, for not all carpets pulled the rug from beneath your feet. Another possibility was Merlin had taken a shine to Benjamin Blackstone, but which Merlin? Merlin the Magician, a wizard in a lot of people's eyes, or John Joseph Merlin, the mechanical wizard, magician of clockwork wonders?

Benjamin was fast asleep so he could not have heard the tick-tock whirling sound of what sounded like a mechanical marvel in the form of a magic carpet turn on a sixpence in the attic and fly out of the bedroom window into the magic shop on the other side of the street, Abracadabra Street.

I cannot possibly say which of those imaginings were true; all I can say is, the dream Benjamin was having that night went like clockwork, a clockwork magic carpet, now that really was a marvel of mechanical wizardry. Once upon a dream time, Benjamin had dreamed up a story in his sleep entitled 'Curious Cuthbert & the Clockwork Cloud Company'; he wrote it down as soon as he woke up and his English teacher Miss Potter gave him an A star. After this dream, perhaps Benjamin would conjure some more magic, as in the morning, Curious Cuthbert & the Clockwork Cloud Carpet popped out of his head exactly like magic.

As a magician, Benjamin was a failure Grade F the lowest grade one could achieve. However, as a storyteller, he was A star, well perhaps not A star but certainly B+, and perhaps one day he would become an A star writer, a wizard with words, sorry, a magician whose pen would become his magic wand, as Benjamin Blackstone found he had the magic touch after all.

But that moment of magic was for another day; one must always focus on the magic moment one is having at the time one is having it, a magic lantern will only show one slide at a time and for good reason.

To be fair to the modern dreamer, it was harder than ever to live in the moment, especially when most dreamers in the modern world had the attention span of a mayfly. Now if the dreamer had the attention to detail of a magical dragonfly, known in nature as a Time Warper, as they appeared to have a magic lantern in their head, they too would be able to slow the moment down and in doing so would be able to catch the magic moment before it disappeared like a dream in the early morning light.

These were the thoughts of one Benjamin Blackstone, old-school boy, old-school magic man, and one who couldn't do old-school magic for toffees. It seemed this old-school dreamer was suffering the same thing that modern dreamers were suffering from – being too close to the object. A dreamer didn't mind being too close to the dream but one thing they did not wish for was to be too close to the nightmare. Benjamin would wonder when he left Dream Street if he was getting too close to a nightmare, one he could not avoid for all the wishful thinking in the world.

26

Bringing the House (of Cards) Down!

The Wheel of Fortune turned; the question was, was this a Wheel of Fortune or a Wheel of Misfortune? Once again, only time would tell. Time, the greatest of all the illusions, both dark and light magic, a law unto itself.

As Benjamin's father had always told him, 'Let the cards fall where they may and hope to god it's the Fortune Card that is the hand you are dealt and not the card of misfortune, the Death Card, the Grim Reaper.' In life you didn't always reap what you sowed, sometimes you sowed the seeds of your own misfortune, as seeds of doubt grew so wild and out of control like, poison ivy poisoning the mind.

Had Madam Matilda handed Benjamin a poisoned chalice or had she handed him a chalice made of gold? Benjamin and Scarlet awoke to see a golden sunrise so magical, surely this day could only be a magical one, one to live long in the memory. A truly golden moment, a magic lantern slide moment to be shown over and over again on the magic lantern of the mind. Benjamin knew he must master the art of mind over matter if he was not to once again fluff his lines. He desperately wanted to rid himself of the tag World's Worst Magician, perhaps today would be that day he would finally be able to perform magic.

'I know what you're thinking, Benjamin,' said Scarlet as she linked arms with Benjamin and they stepped onto the biggest stage of all, Abracadabra Street.

'You do? Please tell me because I don't, I'm a bag of nerves. I can't tell my knee from my elbow; I wish I had a magic carpet bag like Mary Poppins,' sighed Benjamin, still under the rainbow with not a moon bow in sight.

'You're up to your old tricks again – wishful thinking. Today isn't a day for wishful thinking; today is a day for wish fulfilment,' smiled Scarlet, and as she did, Benjamin found himself mirroring the look upon Scarlet's face. He might not be able to do magic all on his own but with some help from a girl who had a magical smile, perhaps, just perhaps, he might be able to.

The big day came for the street party to end all street parties, a street magic party, but unlike most party magic often seen in living rooms around the country for children's birthday parties. This street party really did have the magic touch; hardly surprising given the fact it was being held on a street named Abracadabra Street.

'Well, this is the big day, Abracadabra Street's big birthday bash; let's hope we turn out to be the smash hit of the street party magic,' Matilda cried, clearly full of the party spirit already and the sun had only just come up. Benjamin had only ever seen the sun in one position in the sky, like a giant star, and the moon in the same position, both at different ends of the street, as if in the position these two heavenly bodies would be in at wintertime in the morning, the moon being almost invisible until it popped up, almost as if out of thin air to the keen observer, a stargazer perhaps.

If a rain and a moon bow appeared on the street at the same time, Benjamin would not have been in the least bit surprised: Mother Nature's natural bunting draped over the street, a most magical bunting indeed. And for the final touches, as the night fell on Abracadabra Street, a magical aurora, the icing on the giant birthday cake. That was unless the night fell and the street collapsed under the weight of all the stars and heavenly bodies in the night sky; dark magic indeed.

'I feel like I've been suffering from stage fright all my life but today I feel on top of the world,' Benjamin proclaimed to anyone who would listen, as he felt as if he was walking on air. If the street had decided to take to the air like a giant magic carpet, feeling this grand party should have a setting befitting of it, then he may well be walking on illuminated air on Star Street.

'I feel exactly the same way, the butterflies have been growing bigger and bigger, so much so, I felt as if I might go through some sort of magical metamorphosis from human to butterfly and fly away,' Scarlet smiled as Matilda, Scarlet and Benjamin linked arms, as if about to break into song in a magical musical routine.

The children could not help but laugh to see some of the greatest magicians and conjurers in the world performing simple party magic. Harry Houdini was attempting to conjure up a giant pink elephant out of thin air, with a little bit of help from rubber balloons.

'Hey, Harry, we'll all be seeing pink elephants by the end of this day!' Robert Houdin cried, another pink balloon popping in Houdini's hands.

In the end, Robert Houdin, aka the King of the Conjurers and far better at sleight-of-hand tricks, stepped in and in no time at all there was a whole zoo full of animals, tigers, lions, giraffes, elephants, monkeys, all the colours of the rainbow floating in the air.

'Now that's what I call animal magic!' cried Thurston, aka the Great Magician, who was juggling magic wands and doing it badly as one almost took his eye out.

'Hey, Harry, pull us another rabbit out of the hat, I'm bursting to see some real magic!' chortled Carter, aka the Mysterious, almost bursting with laughter to see the master magician Harry Houdini brought to tears by a simple balloon.

'Not wishing to burst your bubble, Harry, but you should try escaping out of a giant balloon; that's more your bag than party magic,' cried the Maharaja of Magic, suddenly appearing on the street on his magic carpet, as he passed Houdini a carpet bag. 'You'll find all you need in there to perform the trick, including an Indian rope for the Indian Rope Trick, for when the giant balloon bursts, you are going to need it!'

'That's a dirty trick, Maharaja, you've given the game away!' Carter laughed as he spun a plate on the tip of his finger before it fell to the ground and broke into several large pieces.

'A giant hot air balloon? It will be a piece of cake,' retorted Harry Houdini, removing a red paper party hat off his head and producing a large cake out of it just to prove he could do party magic if he put his brilliant magical mind to it.

'I see you've still got the magic touch, Harry,' Thurston grinned, for on the cake written in blue and yellow icing were the words 'Happy Birthday Abracadabra Street'. Benjamin was wondering if Harry Houdini was going to reproduce the old Lewis Carroll trick of passing the cake round first and cutting it later?

The party went by in somewhat of a blur as magical moments came and went in the blinking of an eye, then time seemed to stop for it was time for Matilda and her two young magical protégés to take to the stage. A hushed silence fell over the street. Scarlet and Benjamin wondered if Madam Matilda had gone rather overboard with the publicity having pulled every string she could pull and called in every favour using her very considerable charm to get her way. Matilda's new act was hardly a household name yet it topped the bill. Benjamin wondered if Madam Matilda had more power than she let on, for she appeared to be holding all the cards and one of the cards Benjamin was sure was the Fortune Card from a pack of giant Tarot Cards.

Perhaps this magical world really had been turned upon its head as the bottom-of-the-bill act Benjamin and Scarlet became top of the bill, leaving the two greatest magicians and illusionists of all time, Robert Houdin and Harry Houdini, bottom of the bill. The great magic men were simply support acts or warm-up acts for the two young pretenders to the crown of the World's Greatest Magician. Benjamin Blackstone was a pretender all right, the Great Pretender, pretending he could do magic when he clearly could not. How on earth could Madam Matilda have seen a great magician in him was frankly beyond belief, yet still she appeared to have belief in him, so he must at least try and believe in himself, for Scarlet, Madam Matilda and himself.

The previous night, Matilda and the maker of the magic act, Mr Banini, had wheeled the giant book onto the street under the cover of darkness on the back of a glass funeral carriage, of all things. Thankfully, Benjamin and Scarlet had no knowledge of this, otherwise they would have been forgiven for thinking their fortune (misfortune?) was not the same as Madam Matilda's fortune, and if this act went well she would make a small fortune.

'Ladies and gentlemen, I'll skip the boys and girls, for most are now in bed and if they are not, they should be.' Madam Matilda laughed at her own joke as the street erupted with laughter. It was like being inside a giant vaudeville theatre house, except in this case the roof had been removed, or raised, as in the applause and laughter raised the roof!

'She appears to have the audience in the palm of her hands,' whispered Scarlet as she turned to Benjamin; both of the children were waiting quietly in the wings. The wings in this case were below stage and above a giant popup book waiting to pop up as if by magic, perhaps exactly by magic. The audience appeared to be under Madam Matilda's spell; they might well have been under the influence of moonshine, intoxicated both by liquor and by the rays of a magical golden full moon. Madam Matilda continued with her patter and as she did, the laughter and applause grew, as did her confidence. Soon, she would be ten-foot-tall, perhaps taller; a giant puppet master working her puppets, puppets made of flesh and blood.

'Let's hope we're in safe hands,' grunted Benjamin who was beginning to feel uneasy and this, for once, was not due to stage fright, for something else was troubling him, his sixth sense working overtime.

'Abracadabra!' Matilda cried theatrically as the giant black cloth covering the stage flew off into the air and, as it did, a giant book popped up full of figures, shadowy figures, as still as statues.

'Bravo, bravo!' cried the audience as one voice, standing on tables, chairs, some even hanging out of the windows of their shops. Abracadabra St had seen a lot of magic over the years but nothing quite like this.

'And for my next trick,' Matilda continued, using every trick in the magic book but doing it with such style and humour, it felt to the audience as if they were hearing these well-worn lines for the first time. Matilda waved a giant magic wand as, one by one, the stationary figures came to life. If there had been a glass ceiling on Abracadabra Street, as the architect Sir Joseph Paxton had imagined for streets of the city of London, then the glass ceiling would surely have been shattered. The glass ceiling had become one of the most overused phrases in Benjamin's world, so much so, it had almost lost its meaning. The glass ceiling had certainly lost its magic as had the phrase, 'We're so far through the looking glass.'

If Benjamin was so far through the looking glass, nobody but Alice and the Hatter had been further, and as for the glass ceiling, well, he must have smashed that to smithereens the moment he stepped into this magical space. In truth, he rather fell into this space and that's when Benjamin imagined he'd smashed the looking glass and the glass ceiling at the exact same moment, a magical moment whether he was aware of it or not at the time. Benjamin had imagined if he'd climbed up a very long ladder he would be able to climb out of the book back into the attic and his world. More wishful thinking, or so Benjamin imagined, for if that were true, why didn't the magicians travelling above the magic shops on their magic carpet ever say they had seen another world beyond Abracadabra Street? Maybe because that world was a large empty, dusty attic; to those who saw it, they may well imagine it as a desert or a desolate wasteland.

'I think we've brought the house down!' hissed Benjamin turning to Scarlet.

'As long as we haven't brought it down on our own heads,' grimaced Scarlet as she glanced up when perhaps she should have been glancing down, for the moment she spoke, the two children heard a loud whirring sound followed by what sounded like a giant clock being overwound. A loud crack followed those two alarming sounds as the stage folded up. The truth was, it was the giant popup book that had folded. Snapped shut was the more likely story. The audience was sure this was part of the trick as another loud round of applause rang throughout the street.

'Help, help!' Scarlet and Benjamin cried out in horror as their small world collapsed around their ears but alas, nobody could hear their cries under the thunderous applause. Matilda appeared to have vanished into thin air. Was this also a part of the trick? If it was, it must have been a last-minute add-on, unscripted, improvised, unless Matilda had kept this part of the act to herself in case something went horribly wrong.

'Don't panic, this… this is probably all a part of the trick,' stuttered Scarlet, not sure she believed this to be true.

'I think I know how Harry Houdini felt in the Buried Alive trick when he started to run out of air,' Benjamin groaned, feeling the weight of the world on his shoulders. The book appeared still to be in the stages of collapsing around their ears and to Benjamin it felt as if he was back in his great-grandfather's house, which appeared to be permanently on the verge of collapse and a haunted house to boot.

'It's a pity there isn't a bell in here we could ring, like the ones they put in coffins in case the person in the coffin was still alive,' Scarlet groaned, trying to hold the wooden structure up to stop it crushing them both to death.

Benjamin thought of the line by Charles Dickens from his novel *A Tale of Two Cities*: 'It was the best of times, it was the worst of times.' Well, perhaps he'd had the best of times and now he was having the worst of times, worse than worst of times! It was said that, in times of danger, we find strength we did not know we had, both mental and physical strength. Benjamin wished he had the strength of Hercules or Atlas or a big friendly giant, even an ogre that always wanted to lend a helping hand. Where was Hagrid the giant when you needed him? Giving Benjamin the cold shoulder, turning his back on him, being an ex-wizard, as it was clear that Benjamin Blackstone was being excommunicated by the wizarding community!

It wasn't just the wizards standing up in the audience, which Benjamin imagined were applauding his demise; it was Mr Wizenbaum holding up a Tarot Card, the Death Card, with a picture of the Grim Reaper on it. Both the Reaper and Mr Wizenbaum along with the whole wizarding community were all smiles, crooked smiles at that.

Benjamin saw another smiling face in his mind's eye: it was Madam Matilda and in her hand she too was holding up a Tarot Card – the Fool – what a fool he'd been. Madam Matilda had taken him for a fool, fooled him and Scarlet, pulled the wool over their eyes, deceived them. She pretended to believe in Benjamin, showered him with praise, built him up as a young pretender to the throne of great magicians. Then Madam Matilda had pulled the rug from underneath his feet, torn his playhouse down like a house of cards, Tarot Cards.

A loud creaking noise could be heard, like a giant door in a giant's haunted house; this was followed by the crashing sound of the stage and the giant popup book as it collapsed. This time, there was silence as a deathly hush fell over the street followed by cries of, 'Get them out, get them out!'

27

A Dirty Trick

It took some time for the good folk of Abracadabra Street to pull the large heavy wooden structure off so they could get to where Benjamin and Scarlet were lying. One man said they looked like two sleeping angels, another said it appeared they were asleep. It appeared to the onlookers of this horror show that the children had passed onto the other side. Benjamin and Scarlet's bodies were carried out of the rubble and placed upon the tables that had been set up for the street party.

Then a large shadow appeared and stood over the children; as everybody moved back, an onlooker may have imagined this man to be some kind of Jesus figure – some scholars said Jesus was a magician of sorts. The man took out a pack of playing cards – this seemed a rather odd thing to do – asking the children to pick a card, any card, half expecting their spirits to rise up out of their lifeless bodies and pick a card. It soon became clear the man was holding a deck of Tarot Cards; he shuffled them using only one hand, party magic, nothing more, then held out the deck at arm's length. A few moments later, after keeping the audience in suspense, a Tarot Card slid out of the pack. It was the Fortune Card; if this was a trick, it was a cruel one.

As the crowd around the Tarot Card Conjurer began to murmur their disapproval at this tasteless act of showmanship, Benjamin blinked not once, not twice, but three times, then sat bolt upright as if somebody had sent a surge of electricity through his body. Benjamin stared wild-eyed at the people gathered around him in what seemed like a giant magic circle. Scarlet blinked, once, twice, three times, then sat bolt upright as the two children sat on the table like two ventriloquists' dummies in some kind of macabre horror film.

'Welcome back.' The Tarot Card Conjurer smiled, a crooked smile, as the street erupted, for you see, they were now sure this had all be a part of the act, the third and final part of the act, three being the magic number. The first part of the act, it now became crystal clear, had a false bottom.

'I've never been away, oh, and one more corny line, my death has been greatly exaggerated,' said Benjamin in an automatic fashion.

'This time we brought the house down in a good way.' Scarlet smiled, turning her head towards Benjamin.

'Timing for a magician is everything and so are a magician's instinct; when things go wrong on stage and in life you simply have to make it up as you go along,' Benjamin replied, offering Scarlet his hand... although not in marriage, you understand; after all, Benjamin was only twelve. On the stroke of the following midnight, Benjamin would be thirteen – unlucky for some, for others, well, thirteen is seen as a lucky number, a very lucky number. For a moment that was anything but magical, Benjamin had felt his number was up and now it looked for all the world, a magical world, he was on the up.

Benjamin's instincts for magic had finally come to the fore, in a manner of speaking, or had he just lucked into the magic on this magical street, Abracadabra Street? Either way, Benjamin Blackstone was alive to tell the tale, and what a tale. It would make a great story, from World's Worst Magician to World's Greatest Magician overnight, literally an overnight success.

Benjamin saw the Fool Card from the Tarot deck appear in his mind's eye and his smiled; yes, he knew he was fooling himself, but the Fool Card in the Tarot deck was one of the most useful cards in the pack and was used more than any other card. After all, a magician had to use every trick in the book to fool the audience and at times fool himself into believing he really was the Greatest Magician in the World, any world. Self-belief was the key, the magic key; it unlocked all the doors, magic wardrobes, gates, magic cabinets, treasure chests and magic trunks, which contained all the magic tricks one needed to perform on the greatest stage of all: the Theatre of Life.

'I have to say, it did cross my mind you were a part of Matilda's Magic Act, her partner in magic crime, the crime of the century, this Victorian century,' Benjamin said, trying to get to the bottom of this magical mystery without accusing Scarlet of being in cahoots with Madam Matilda.

'And it did cross my mind you were Madam Matilda's stooge,' Scarlet replied, sure Benjamin was cross-questioning her like the great detective Sherlock Holmes. 'It seems Madam Matilda was in debt up to her eyeballs, one of which I'm sure was made of glass and the other one bloodshot with a patch over it,' Scarlet grunted, kicking a pebble across the street, clearly annoyed with herself for letting Madam Matilda pull the wool over her eyes.

'It looks like we've both been used. Madam Matilda must have seen more than we'd realised when she found us that night in the attic,' said Benjamin, as the drama unfolded and the inquests began. 'We should go after her, confront her; get the book back in the wrong hands and it could turn this and every other world upside down and inside out!'

'She's worked us like a couple of puppets, pulling our strings, and what's worse, we can't confront her; she'll be halfway round the world by now,' Scarlet sighed, imagining Madam Matilda was on a magical street in Timbuktu or Constantinople using the Victorian popup book to astound, wow and amaze as part of her new one-woman magic show, one that would see her as the World's Greatest Magician.

'Fate will catch up with her one day, that's how the world works: what goes around comes around, especially in a magic circle. The circle will close in around her and when it does, she will get what she deserves,' grunted Benjamin with a steely look of determination in his eyes.

Halfway around the world or, the more likely story, halfway around Abracadabra Street…

*

'I think I'll stop here for the night. I would imagine by the time everyone has realised I've done a magical disappearing act, it will be too late for them to do anything about it,' cackled Madam Matilda, sounding like all three witches gathered around a boiling caldron from Shakespeare's tragedy *Macbeth*.

'Now, let's see just how magical you are, my little magical book, although please don't try any black magic and take my eye out. Time for a little bit of magic, or should I say big-time magic? As they say, big things come in small packets,' Matilda added, rubbing her hands in glee at the prospect of the wheel of fortune finally turning her way.

Madam Matilda laid the Victorian popup book out on the grass and waited for the magic show to begin.

'Fireworks, I do so love a good fireworks display!' Matilda cried, leaning over the book as if she imagined she had gone back to her childhood when a simple fireworks display seemed the most magical thing ever. What Madam Matilda saw was indeed a most magical and dazzling display of magic from the miniature magicians on Abracadabra Street, or should I say the miniature version of Abracadabra Street, for Madam Matilda was still on Abracadabra Street. All magicians that had ever walked the boards performing their acts of magic had stepped upon this magical street at one time or the other, all the greats, Merlin the Magician; Robert Houdin, the King of Conjurers; Harry Houdini, the Master Magician and Escapologist. Yet, up until now, this moment, a magical moment in the eyes of Madam Matilda, there had never been a great female magician. Madam Matilda saw her name up in lights; it was written in the stars, she was to be that magician, or 'magicianess', as Matilda imagined her meteoric rise to stardom.

A shadow appeared on the street. Where it had come from, Matilda was not sure. She imagined for a second it too had popped out of the book and now it was looming large over both her and the Victorian popup book. Matilda wondered further if this was a different spin on the old Jinn in the bottle routine – once out of the bottle, the Jinn could never be put back in. Was this the same old story, replacing the shadow and the book for the Jinn and the bottle?

'Shadow Conjurer, what do you want? Perhaps… perhaps you wish for me to grant you three wishes? A turn-up for the book, *A Thousand and One Nights*. Alas, I am no Jinn,' laughed Matilda uproariously, brushing the shadow aside in a dismissive manner. The shadow would not be dismissed so easily; in fact, it grew to three times its size, blocking out the moonlight as the street fell into darkness. Then another shadow appeared on the street, as if a party of another kind was about to begin: a funeral party – Madam Matilda's funeral party – as a ghostly New Orleans jazz band appeared on the street.

'Pick a card, any card, as long as it's this one,' laughed the shadow so loudly, Matilda felt as if her eardrums would burst at any moment.

'I don't like cheap cards tricks, never have!' spat Matilda, this time trying to walk straight through the shadow as if it wasn't there. But Madam Matilda found she could not walk through this shadow; she fell violently backwards as if she had just hit a brick wall.

'Welcome to the world of wishful thinking,' the shadow laughed in manic fashion. 'Well then, pick one of my cards, the deck is not loaded,' the shadow cried, holding a pack of Tarot Cards out. It felt to Madam Matilda as if the two shadows were also performing on Abracadabra Street. Madam Matilda did not believe the shadows; she sensed both of the decks they were holding were loaded and with only one card: the Grim Reaper, the Death Card.

The two shadows suddenly vanished but the Tarot Cards did not; they grew larger and larger then flew towards Matilda, knocking her sideways as she stumbled, tripped and fell into the book. By this time, the Victorian popup book entitled *Abracadabra Street* appeared to be up to its old tricks as the book was now ten times its original size.

All the while the shadows had been practising their dark conjuring tricks with the Tarot Card, the magic show in the book had continued, so much so, you could hardly see the action for smoke. As for the mirrors, 'All smoke and mirrors', another catchphrase used in magic circles, the street was lined with them, all blackened by the smoke so the glass in the looking glasses was as black as coal-smoke glass. The mirrors cracked, causing splinters to fly everywhere Matilda was now lying on the street, her eyes bleeding badly and, worse still, her dress was now ablaze. Suddenly, the book slammed shut as a muffled cry died in Matilda's throat like in a nightmare, a cry that nobody heard, 'Help me, please!'

The giant shadows Matilda had named the Shadow Conjurers had by now reappeared, as had the moon, as the Victorian popup book named *Abracadabra Street* shrank until it was back to its original size. Then the shadows merged to become one giant shadow; the shadow sauntered over to where the book lay, bent down and put the book into himself. Or this is how it must have appeared if anybody had been watching the dark magic show. The shadow no doubt was wearing a black tunic or frockcoat of some kind; perhaps the shadow was a wizard, a wizard of all things on Abracadabra Street, best he disappeared as fast as he could before he was chased out of town a town called Abracadabra.

As the shadow departed from the scene, it split into two, one shadow going one way, the other shadow going the other. It was clear one of the shadows was a shadow conjured by the magic of moonlight, while the other shadow was conjured by the magic of the sun. At least this was how it would have appeared to a lone figure looking on as the shadow stepped out of the shadows, as daylight shone on one side of the street while moonlight shone upon the other side of the street. 'Well, I cannot say I didn't see this coming, although I suppose I didn't,' the man chortled to himself, then added dryly, 'Merlin the Magician, perhaps you are not so great as you and everybody else imagines you are; perhaps it really is simply a case of all smoke and mirrors.'

*

Some small time later...

'I have some sad news, children, no, perhaps I need to rephrase that – I have some bad news and as we all know bad news travels fast, so perhaps you have already heard this news,' Mr Wizenbaum said, shuffling his Tarot Cards with one hand as one card appeared out of the pack, the Death Card with the depiction of the Grim Reaper on it. As soon as Benjamin saw this card, he gasped, fearing the worst, perhaps even worse than worst, as Mr Wizenbaum confessed he had been a wizard all the time. After which, Mr Wizenbaum waved a magic wand over Benjamin, turning him into a warty toad, and warty toads being said to be rather delicious with roast chestnuts on Abracadabra Street, Mr Wizanbaum polished him off in no time at all! All the wizards on Abracadabra Street then appeared out of the shadows and carried Mr Wizenbaum off on their shoulders, cheering loudly and throwing their wizards' hats into the air.

'Have no fear, my boy, this card does not have your name on it, nor yours, Scarlet. It does, however, have a name written on it in invisible ink, or so I imagine: the name of Madam Matilda,' Mr Wizenbaum continued with a face as straight as a coffin lid as Benjamin blew out his cheeks in relief.

'Wh... what happened?' gasped Benjamin and Scarlet as one, although inside they had mixed emotions, still not sure what to believe and what not to believe. Benjamin had always pictured Mr Wizenbaum as the pantomime villain on Abracadabra Street and Matilda as Cinderella, Snow White and Rapunzel all rolled into one.

'Madam Matilda died in a fire,' Mr Wizanbaum replied, not wishing to share all the gory details of what had happened to Matilda or how he knew the full story. 'No doubt in the Penny Dreadfuls and Penny Peculiars, they will say she suffered a case of Spontaneous Human Combustion or died while testing out one of her fantastical illusions.'

Benjamin did not need to know the full story; he could imagine the full story, or at least he imagined he could – several full stories, in fact, enough to fill a whole book. The two stories that popped out of his head almost simultaneously were the ones in which either Mr Wizenbaum put a spell on Madam Matilda, shrinking her, after which he slipped her into the book as if she were a page marker and then slammed the book shut, crushing her to death. The other short horror story, half inspired by the Brothers Grimm, the other half by the American gothic writer Edgar Allen Poe, was Atticus Blackstone, his great-grandfather's spirit, which had been trapped in the book, popped up and finally did the right thing before 'leaving stage left', as they say in theatrical circles. Or on this occasion, magic circles, if Abracadabra Street was indeed a circular street – or was that his half-brother Nathan?

Neither of these Victorian horror stories were true, for a little bird whispered something in Benjamin's ear telling him the truth, this bird was not an owl, wise or otherwise, but a nightjar. 'Madam Matilda sold your family down the river,' hissed the nightjar, then the next moment it had vanished, to be replaced by a man standing upon a magic carpet. It was the Maharaja of Magic, the man who owned the magic carpet shop down the street, a man able to change his appearance at the drop of a hat. The Maharaja of Magic then disappeared leaving only the magic carpet hanging in the air. Benjamin imagined the magician had turned himself into an even more magical carpet, which disappeared into the stars.

The Finale

The Magic Trunk of the Mind

Mr Wizenbaum then reappeared, as if by dark magic, and winked at Benjamin for some strange reason. Benjamin blinked three times, his eyes like the tiny shutters of a Victorian box camera, as Mr Wizenbaum reappeared across the opposite side of the street and winked at Benjamin for the second time in as many moments. It was almost as if Mr Wizenbaum had the ability to be in two places at once, as if he was a part of a double act, his own double act. Now he came to think of it, Mr Wizenbaum's appearance did look overly theatrical, as if he was wearing a wig, and his face had been covered in white powder as often used in stage productions.

Surely not? No, that was ridiculous, thought Benjamin, laughing to himself, for he was imagining Mr Wizenbaum the trickster was his great-grandfather, Atticus Blackstone. But it didn't end there, this wild imagining, for Mr Wizenbaum was also his great-uncle, Nathan Blackstone, Atticus Blackstone's half-brother. It was true, one thing could be in two places and space at the same time. According to the quantum magicians, M theory, also known as Magic Theory, stated there were eleven dimensions, not just the four that we humans have all grown up believing was the truth.

Whatever the truth, Benjamin felt his story in this world had reached its natural conclusion; well, perhaps not natural conclusion, more like unnatural conclusion. But as the great detective Sherlock Holmes was so fond of saying, 'When you have dismissed all the evidence, whatever is left, however unnatural, is the truth.' Now Benjamin may have twisted Mr Sherlock Holmes' words somewhat but not so much that they did not ring true, at least in the ears of one Master Benjamin Blackstone, Esq of no fixed abode, at least not in this Victorian world.

The ringing in the ears was like music to Benjamin's ears, for a magician was performing the magic rings, also known as miracle rings, within spitting distance of where he was standing. There was also a woman playing the crystal goblets, wetting her finger and running it around the rims of the goblets to make the sweetest sounds imaginable. Benjamin bowed to everybody on this magical street, then bowed to the street itself, then bowed for the final time, as if to an encore on stage, to one magic shop in particular, Blackstone Magic. Two men in the shop bowed back to him and then disappeared as if… exactly… well, I'll leave the rest up to your imagination.

'I think this is where we both say goodbye,' said Benjamin with a heavy heart as he looked Scarlet in the eye.

'The natural end, I would imagine. I saw it coming in my dreams. You might say it's time for both of us to spread our wings and fly, as time flies; none of us knows when we are destined to reach our end. The end I have imagined for myself is to become one of the greatest magicians of all time, man or woman, and for you, Benjamin, well, I imagine you wish to return to your own little world.' Scarlet smiled as if she had a crystal ball in her head or perhaps that should be book – a Victorian crystal popup book – as Benjamin was now imagining. Perhaps Scarlet was having the same thought, for it really did appear as if the two young people could read one another's minds, or at least they could read one another's imaginations.

'I wish you all the best, although I don't think you will need my good wishes or anybody else's.' Benjamin smiled, shaking Scarlet firmly by the hand, trying not to let his emotions get the better or the worst of him. Scarlet shook Benjamin's hand, a tear not far away, as Benjamin took a white handkerchief out of his pocket fully intending to give to Scarlet to wipe her eyes. However, what actually happened was anything but magical as a pack of cards, a white dove and various magical knickknacks spilled out of Benjamin's pocket and onto the street.

'And I still can't do magic, it's official. In whatever world I am in, I am the World's Worst Magician, worse than worse magician!' Benjamin laughed as did Scarlet and, despite everything, this seemed the perfect ending.

'Better go, time waits for no magician, man or woman, and we don't want to flood Abracadabra Street, imagine that,' Scarlet said, forcing a smile onto her face.

'I'll try not to imagine it or anything else for the rest of my life as the magic is clearly inside my head, has been all along, in my head but not in my hands.' Benjamin smiled and as he did, without any help from magic whatsoever, a smile appeared on Scarlet's face, lighting up the whole street.

'Three cheers for magic!' cried Scarlet, determined to upstage Benjamin with a little street magic for old times' sake. You see, two glasses appeared to be floating on a carpet of air. Scarlet reached for the two glasses, full to the brim and overflowing with moonshine, and passed one to Benjamin. 'One for you one for me, cheers,'

'Old time street magic, you gotta love it, the oldest tricks in the magic book, the Floating Glass Trick plus the Iota Bowl Trick; the trick to magic is whatever you want it to be,' laughed Benjamin, high on the magic of life, as Scarlet disappeared into thin air, as did Benjamin Blackstone.

To those working their magic on the street, they did not seem to notice a moon bow one end of the street and a rainbow at the other end and in the middle, an aurora, a green, blue and purple curtain. Benjamin stepped into the curtain and vanished into thin air; the last thing he heard was a stationmaster crying out and blowing his tin whistle, 'Last train to Abracadabra Street.' It seemed once again Benjamin Blackstone had missed the steamboat, the omnibus, the magic carpet ride and the last train to Abracadabra Street. But this time round, he was happy to miss these magical forms of transport, for he was sure that, one day, they would come around again, just like a giant magic circle.

*

The next thing Benjamin Blackstone knew, was he was back in the attic, the Victorian popup book entitled *Abracadabra Street* by his side; the book was closed. Benjamin walked over to the book, picked it up and tried to open it. But the book would not open so he tried the magic word, 'Open sesame!' That did not do the trick either, so Benjamin tried another magic word, 'Abracadabra!', sure he would soon have to add yet another magical phrase to this lexicon of magic words in his head by crying out, 'Hey presto!' However, as the book did not open, the words 'Hey presto' stayed locked inside his head.

Benjamin did not scowl or throw the book down in temper, quite the opposite. The smile he left on Abracadabra Street and in Scarlet's capable hands returned, a smile wider than a mile, wider than an upturned rainbow or a moon bow, perhaps even wider than Abracadabra Street itself.

All right, perhaps that is pushing the magic a little too far beyond the imagination, beyond the rainbow, even the moon bow, or perhaps not. Magic, like the imagination, could and would stretch and stretch and stretch, yet it would never break; magic was unbreakable. Even when the universe ended, the magic would still be there, invisible, naturally enough, and when the time was right there would be a repeat showing in this vast Theatre of Magic. Perhaps Benjamin and Scarlet would be reunited when this fantastic piece of magic occurred, in another form, no doubt, as the magic dust once again worked its magic, reforming, transforming, working its magic.

Whichever world we were in, magic was all around us, as was nature, if only we used our eyes and our senses, which included our sixth sense.

Benjamin picked the book up, went over to the small door in the attic, placed the book back where he had found it in the battered old trunk with the travel labels from all over the world, or all over Abracadabra Street, then closed the door. He then covered the wall with some old wallpaper.

Perhaps one day someone else would come across the book in the attic hidden away and when they did they too may find themselves on a magical street named Abracadabra

Street. In the meantime, the good folk of Abracadabra Street were sure to entertain themselves with extraordinary feats of magic that would make most people's toes curl and hair stand upon end like fairy sparks.

Benjamin left the magical space of the attic and the old house, turning his back on magic and the family magic business, or so it appeared. But once again, appearances can be deceiving, especially in circles where magic is practised. You see, Benjamin became a writer, or moreover a storyteller of old-school magic – not a school for wizards, I hasten to add, there wasn't much room in Benjamin's books for wizards – it was old-time magic all the way. Benjamin's first book was entitled *Abracadabra Street*; the follow-up was a one-word title, the magic word as it happens: *Abracadabra*. This magical tale was about a town called Abracadabra set in a giant magic circle, a carousel which could appear and disappear from one place and space to another, a most magical space, anywhere in time and space in fact.

Facts have their time and place even in books of a fictional nature, but it's the fictions we readers so love and storytellers so love to twist, but not like a party magician, twisting a green balloon into a poor-man's dragon.

Benjamin never did get to be a great magician; in fact, he didn't even get to perform a great trick in or out of Abracadabra Street, or at least so it appeared. However, life and magic can be most deceiving, as the whole time Benjamin was on this magical street he was creating magic, storing it up in his head to later turn into a story of a most magical nature. The magic really is inside your own head, a magic trunk with at least three false bottoms, three being the magic number.

Benjamin Blackstone was happy to stay in the shadows, he did not mind gaslight, candlelight or the light of the beam of a magic lantern being shone above him from a distance, but a spotlight still made him want to disappear into the attic of his mind, where he felt most comfortable. Benjamin moved into Atticus Blackstone's house, or moreover his attic, for that was where he conjured up his most magical stories. And all the while a stone's throw away sat a magical book, a magical world, one that perhaps one day he would reread, perhaps even re-enter. A book with only one double page – if any writer could conjure up an unforgettable story using only one double page they really would have to be the most magical of storytellers, wouldn't they?

The family magic business, Blackstone Magic, did not fold up like a giant pack of cards, playing cards or Tarot Cards, or a Victorian popup book, without the prodigal son Benjamin Blackstone to guide it through troubled times. In fact, Blackstone Magic thrived as it did on Abracadabra Street, or so Benjamin further imagined. This was in no small way thanks to Benjamin's books on the topic of magic, as old-school magic in the theatres all across the country came back into fashion big time. Benjamin imagined his great-grandfather Atticus Blackstone had finally gone towards the light as had his half-brother Nathan, who appeared by his side all smiles. The light Benjamin imagined was a giant stage light, the beam of a giant magic lantern in a rather grand and magical theatre named Heaven, a fanciful notion, I'll grant you, but one Benjamin rather liked.

The mansion house Atticus Blackstone left in his will to the Blackstone family Benjamin turned into the Museum of Old-Time Magic, for he was quite happy living and working in the attic space where he performed his best magic. Later, Benjamin turned the attic into the Attic Theatre, a most magical theatre indeed and one all the great magicians from the modern era played in. When the lights were turned out in the old mansion house, a light could still be seen shining in the attic, candlelight naturally, unless an unlit magic phantasmagorical lantern as if by magic turned itself on as the old-time magicians came back for one more magical variety performance. Or so Benjamin imagined, as the magic left his head, flowed through his arms into his fingers as, for the first time in his own time, he really did appear to have the magic touch.

Not all books about magic were magical; the word 'magic' did not necessarily mean magic had been at work at the time they were written. Benjamin's stories, however, appeared to have that magic touch. It was as if as soon as you opened his books, the magic popped out, as did the characters, taking you to a magical place and space. And this magic did not leave your mind until you shut the book up after reading the last page, and even then, the magic did not leave, as if a repeat performance was going on in the shadows of your mind without your knowledge.

Benjamin could never tell anybody in his world the real true story of his great-grandfather and his great-uncle's fantastical lives – Nathan, black as the Ace of Spades, Atticus, as white as a ghost – because understandably nobody would have believed a word of it. However, as a storyteller, he could tell the fictional version of their life stories hidden within the pages of a fictional storybook entitled *Abracadabra Street*.

Magic is only magic when it happens once in a blue moon – any more than that and magic itself loses its magic, leaving out elves for the foreseeable future!

The End...

If you enjoyed *Abracadabra Street* then you may well enjoy the follow-up, *Abracadabra*, set in the town of Abracadabra, which keeps appearing and disappearing off the magic map exactly like magic. Benjamin Blackstone, wizard with words (sorry, wash my mouth out with carbolic soap!), master magician of the written word (Abracadabra) returns on another magical adventure and misadventure to astound and amaze. There may even be a maze made of moonstone in the town of Abracadabra, clear and crystalline; it, like the town of Abracadabra, cannot be seen until you walk right into it… dark magic indeed… or walk right through it… if you are a great magician, the moonstone gate entrance, for it knows the difference between a wizard and a man of magic, a magician.

Other Titles by Mark Roland Langdale

Professor Doppelganger and the Fantastical Cloud Factory
Animal Alchemy
The (Phantasmagorical) Astrarium Compendium
The Clock People
The Time Travellers Club
The Toy Museum